G. J. Pledger 1:

PURRFECT CRIME

THE MYSTERIES OF MAX 5

NIC SAINT

PUSS IN PRINT PUBLICATIONS

PURRFECT CRIME

The Mysteries of Max 5

Copyright © 2017 by Nic Saint

Edited by Chereese Graves

www.nicsaint.com

Give feedback on the book at: info@nicsaint.com

facebook.com/nicsaintauthor
@nicsaintauthor

First Edition

Printed in the U.S.A

PROLOGUE

*D*onna Bruce was a woman profoundly in love with herself. From personal experience she knew there was no other person as amazing as she was. She was smart, successful, beautiful, and, above all, she was kind to humans, children and dogs, which cannot be said about everyone. She was a giver, not a taker. In fact she gave so much she often wondered if people appreciated her enough.

Her kids, for instance, could probably love her more for all the sacrifices she had made. For one thing, they'd pretty much ruined her figure. After the twins were born, something strange but not very wonderful had happened to her hips. They'd never looked the same again. And when she saw what breastfeeding did to her boobs, she'd vowed never to fall into that horrible trap again.

She now carefully tucked her golden tresses beneath the pink shower cap, wrapped the white towel embroidered with her company's crest—a nicely rendered tiara—around her perfectly toned and tanned body, and stepped into the sauna cabin. She had the cabin installed only six months ago as a special treat to herself when donna.vip, the lifestyle website she'd launched a decade ago, had topped 200 million in revenue.

She languidly stretched out on the authentic Finnish wood bench, took a sip from her flute of Moët & Chandon Dom Perignon, and closed her eyes. She'd just done a conference call with her CEO and now it was time to relax. Later today she had a session with her private fitness coach scheduled, and to top it all off she was going to treat herself to a healing massage as well. Time to get pampered!

And she'd just reached that slightly drowsy state she enjoyed so much when a soft clanking sound attracted her attention. She opened her eyes and saw through the slight haze that filled the cabin that there was someone moving about outside.

She frowned, wondering who it could be. Her housekeeper Jackie wasn't coming in until ten, and the rest of the staff knew better than to intrude on her alone time. It was hard to make out the person's face, as the one small window was all steamed up. With a grunt of annoyance she got up and wiped her hand across the glass to look out. And that's when she noticed something very disturbing: the person was wearing a mask of some kind. One of those silly Halloween masks.

"What do you think you're doing?" she called out.

But the intruder just stood there, unmoving, staring at her through the black mask that covered his or her entire face.

"Who are you?" she asked. "Answer me at once!"

When the person didn't respond, she shook her head and took a firm grip on the wood door handle, giving it a good yank. The door didn't budge. She tried again, knowing that these sauna doors could be sticky, but to no avail. And that's when she saw that someone—presumably the masked person outside—had stuck a long object through the door's handle, blocking it. It was her long handle loofah, the one she'd intended to take into the sauna with her.

"Hey! This isn't funny!" she cried, tapping the pane furiously. "Open this door right now!"

And that's when the masked figure reacted for the first time by raising a hand and pointing a finger at her, cocking their thumb and making a shooting gesture. And in that exact moment, she became aware of an odd sound that seemed to come from somewhere above her head. A buzzing sound. She looked up in alarm, and when she saw the first dozen bees streaming into the sauna cabin, she uttered a cry of shock and fear.

She rapped the window again, more frantic this time. "Let me out! Why are you doing this to me?! Just let me out of here!"

More bees fluttered into the cramped space and soon started filling it. There must have been hundreds, or maybe even thousands! And as they descended upon her, she felt the first stings. She started swatting them away with her towel, but there were too many of them, and for some reason they seemed drawn to her, whipped into a frenzy by some unknown cause. And as she stumbled and fell, desperately flapping her hands in a bid to get rid of the pesky insects, she soon succumbed. Her final thought, before she lost consciousness was, "Why me?!"

CHAPTER 1

*H*aving spent most of the night outside, looking up at the stars and commenting to Dooley on their curious shape, attending a meeting of cat choir in the nearby Hampton Cove Park, and generally contemplating the state of the world and my place in it, I was ready to perform my daily duty and make sure my human Odelia Poole got a bright and early start on her day. I do this by jumping up onto her bed, plodding across Odelia's sleeping form, and finally kneading her arm until she wakes up and gives me a cuddle. This has been our morning ritual since just about forever.

When I finally reached the top of the stairs, slightly winded, a pleasant sound emanating from the bedroom filled me with a warm and fuzzy feeling of benevolence: Odelia was softly snoring, indicating she was in urgent need of a wake-up catcall. So I padded over, and jumped up onto the foot of the bed. At least, that was my intention, only for some reason I must have misjudged the distance, for instead of landing on all fours on the bed, I landed on my butt on the bedside rug.

I shook my head, happy that no one saw me in this awkward position. With a slight shrug of the shoulders, I decided to try again. This time the result was even worse. I never even cleared the bed frame, let alone the mattress or the comforter. Like an Olympic pole vaulter who discovers he's lost the ability, I suddenly found myself facing a new and horrifying reality: I couldn't jump anymore!

"Hey, Max," a familiar voice sounded behind me. "What are you doing?"

"What does it look like I'm doing, Dooley?" I grumbled. "I'm trying to jump into bed!"

He paused, then asked, "So why are you still on the floor?"

"Because…" I stared up at the bed, which all of a sudden had turned into an insurmountable obstacle for some reason. "Actually I don't know what's going on. The bed just seems higher now."

"A sudden weakness," Dooley decided knowingly. "It happens to me all the time."

"Well, it doesn't happen to me," I said, scratching my head. Yes, cats scratch their heads. We just make sure we retract our claws, otherwise it would be a fine mess.

"You probably need food. Did you have breakfast? When I don't have my breakfast I feel weak. Do you feel weak?"

I gave him my best scowl. "I feel fine. And for your information, yes, I did have my breakfast. The best kibble money can buy and a nice chunk of chicken and liver paté."

"Wow, what happened?"

"What do you mean, what happened?"

"I thought Odelia only got you the cheap stuff? Why did she go out and splurge all of a sudden?"

"I guess she felt I deserved it. I have been helping her solve murder case after murder case lately."

"Me too, but I didn't get any special treats."

"You have to file your complaint with Gran, Dooley. She is your human, after all."

Dooley's Ragamuffin face sagged. "Gran has been too busy to notice me lately."

"Too busy? Why, what's she been up to?"

"Beats me. She's been receiving packages in the mail. A lot of them. In fact Marge and Tex are pretty much fed up with her. Seems like they're the ones who have to pay for all those packages."

Perhaps now would be a good time to make some introductions, especially for the people who haven't been following my adventures closely. My name is Max, as you have probably deduced, and I'm something of a private cat sleuth. Since Odelia is a reporter and always in need of fresh and juicy stories, I'm only too happy to supply them. My frequent collaborator on these outings is Dooley, my best friend and neighbor. Dooley's human is Vesta Muffin, Odelia's grandmother who lives next door. Dooley is my wingcat. My partner in crime. Between you and me, Dooley is not exactly the brightest bulb in the bulb shop, so it's a good thing he's got me. I'm smart enough for the both of us.

"Why don't I give you a paw up?" Dooley asked now.

"I don't know..." I muttered. I glanced behind Dooley, making sure he was alone. If we were going to do this, I didn't want there to be any witnesses.

Dooley followed my gaze. "What are you looking at?" Then he got it. "Oh, if you're looking for Harriet, she was fast asleep in Brutus's paws. Those two must have had a rough night."

My face clouded. Being reminded of Brutus usually has a souring effect on my mood. You see, Brutus is what us cats call an intruder. He came waltzing into our lives a couple of weeks ago and has refused to leave ever since. He belongs to Chase Kingsley, a cop Odelia has taken a liking to, but seems to spend an awful lot of time next door, cozying up to Harriet, Odelia's mom's white Persian.

I made up my mind. "Let's do this," I grunted. If we didn't, Odelia might wake up of her own accord, and I'd miss my window of opportunity to put in some much-needed snuggle time.

Dooley padded up to me and plunked down on his haunches. "How do you want to do this?"

"Simple. I jump and you give me a boost."

"You mean, like, on the count of three or something?"

"Or something." I got ready, poised at the foot of the bed and said, "One—two—"

"Wait," Dooley said. "Are we doing this on three or after three?"

"What do you mean?"

"Do I boost you on three, or right after?"

"Why would you boost me right after? The count of three usually means the count of three, Dooley."

"So, one, two, three and boost? Or one, two, three, pause, and then boost?"

"One, two, three, boost," I said, starting to lose my patience. "Now, are we doing this or not?"

He thought about this for a moment, a puzzled look on his face. "Do you want to do this?"

"Of course I want to do this! Preferably before we die of old age."

Dooley's eyes went wide. "Die of old age? Do you think we're dying, Max?!"

"No, we're not dying! I just want to put in some snuggle time, is that so hard to understand?"

"Oh, right," he said, understanding dawning. "I thought you said we were dying."

For some reason Dooley has been obsessing about dying

lately. Usually I can talk him out of it, but then he sees something on TV and the whole thing starts all over again.

"Are you ready?"

Dooley nodded. "I'm ready, Max."

"One—two—"

"Wait!"

I groaned. "What is it now?"

"Where do I boost you?"

"Up the bed! Where else?"

"No, I mean, do I boost your butt or your hind paws or what? I'm new to this boosting business," he explained apologetically.

"It's not exactly an Olympic discipline, Dooley. There are no rules. You can boost me wherever you want." On second thought… "Though stay away from my butt."

"Right. Stay away from your butt. So where…"

"Anywhere but my butt! Now one—two—"

"Max!"

"What?!"

"What if I boost you too hard and you end up flying across the bed and down the other side?"

I fixed him with a hard look. "Trust me, Dooley, the chances of that happening are slim to none. I mean, look at us. I'm like the Dwayne Johnson of cats and you're more like Andrew Garfield in *Hacksaw Ridge*, all scrawny and mangy. You'll be lucky if you can boost me a couple inches, which is all I need," I hastened to add.

"Do you think I'm too mangy?" asked Dooley with a frown.

"Not too mangy. You're just thin is all. A very healthy thin."

"Not a sickly thin? Like an I'm-about-to-die thin?"

Oh, God. I did not need this aggravation. "Absolutely not.

More like a my-name-is-Gwyneth-Paltrow-and-I'm-willowy-and-gorgeous kind of thin."

"I thought you said I looked like Andrew Garfield?"

"In a very Gwyneth Paltrow-y way."

This seemed to please him, as he gave me a grateful smile. "Why, thanks, Max. That's the nicest thing you've ever said to me."

"Great. Now about that boost?"

"Oh! Right! I forgot all about that."

"Focus, Dooley. Now, are you ready?"

"Ready," he said, his face a study in concentration.

"One—two—three—"

"Boost!" he cried and placed both paws on my butt, giving me a mighty shove.

And… we had liftoff! Only it didn't last very long, nor did it carry me where I was aiming to go. Instead, I plunked right back down again, landing on top of Dooley, who ended up squeezed beneath my sizable buns.

There was a momentary pause, while we both figured out what went wrong, then Dooley croaked, "Can you please lift your butt, Max? You're choking me!"

Applause broke out behind us, and a loud cackling sound, and when I looked up, I saw we'd been joined by Harriet and Brutus. The latter was applauding, a Draco Malfoy-type sneer on his mug, and Harriet was doing the cackling, apparently finding the whole scene hilarious.

"What's so funny?" I asked with an angry look at the newly arrived.

"You!" Brutus cried. "You're so fat you can't even jump on the bed!"

"I'm not fat! I'm just… experiencing some issues with my takeoff."

"Issues with your takeoff! You're not an airplane, Max.

You're a cat. A cat too fat to fly!" Harriet dissolved into giggles while Brutus was laughing so hard his belly shook.

"Max!" Dooley breathed. "You're... choking... me..."

I released Dooley by lifting my butt, then resumed my scowling. "I'm not fat—I'm big-boned. There's a difference. And Odelia probably bought a new bed, that's all. I never had any trouble jumping into the old bed, which was still here yesterday morning. Isn't that right Dooley?"

But Dooley was still catching his breath, taking big gulps of it.

"That's the exact same bed as always," said Brutus. He narrowed his eyes at me. "Girlfriend stealer."

I rolled my eyes. "Here we go again."

Brutus had walked up to me and poked my chest with his paw. "You kissed my girlfriend, Max. I saw you so don't try to deny it."

"I didn't kiss anyone! She kissed me!"

"That's what you say."

"Because that's what happened!"

He leaned in and dropped his voice to a whisper. "I thought we had an understanding, Max. I thought you and I were friends. And then you went and did a thing like that." He pursed his lips. "You're despicable. There's no other word for it."

"I didn't kiss her," I hissed. "She kissed me. I'm not even interested in Harriet!"

"What are you two whispering about?" Harriet asked with a laugh.

"Nothing, honey bunch," said Brutus in his sweetest voice. "Just clearing up some stuff."

"Max is right, Brutus," Dooley loud-whispered. "Harriet kissed him, not the other way around. And he didn't even like it, did you, Max?" These last words were spoken with a look of reproach in my direction. Dooley has always fancied

Harriet, and he cannot grasp being kissed by that divine feline and not enjoying the experience.

"I heard you," said Harriet, tripping up deftly. "And for your information, I didn't kiss Max."

"See?!" Brutus exclaimed triumphantly.

"My Inner Goddess did."

"What?!"

Harriet raised her chin defiantly. "I can't be held responsible for every little thing my Inner Goddess does, Brutus. Sometimes she wears a blindfold. I thought I was kissing you, actually. I only realized my mistake when I reached out and the only thing my paw met was a yielding fluffiness where rock-hard muscles should have been."

Brutus stared at her. "Go on."

She placed a paw on his chest and closed her eyes. "See, now that I'm feeling your steely pecs I know it's you. That was my mistake. I kissed first and touched later."

I groaned loudly. "Yielding fluffiness?!"

"Shut up, Max," said Brutus. "Watch and learn."

And then the two of them locked lips. Instinctively I held up a paw to cover Dooley's eyes. He did not have to see this. He seemed to appreciate the gesture, for he didn't slap my paw away. He only asked, when the smooching sounds finally abated, "Is it over yet?"

"Yes, it is," I said, lowering my paw. Harriet had kissed me, no doubt about it, but if it made her feel better to lie to both herself and to Brutus, it was fine by me. I didn't need Brutus going back to his old bullying ways. This détente we had going for us suited me fine, so I was happy when finally the kissing stopped and Brutus slapped me on the back.

"And that's how you do it, buddy!"

"Great," I muttered. "Now, can you give me a boost? I need to wake up Odelia."

"Sure thing," said Brutus, suddenly in an expansive mood.

And as I got ready to take the leap again, he got into position directly behind me, not unlike a running back. And before I could initiate the launch sequence, Brutus was shouting, "Hut one—hut two—hut three—go!"

I made the mighty jump and... "Owowowow!" Brutus, instead of giving me a regular boost, had dug his nails into my behind! The result was that I flew up onto the bed and landed right on top of Odelia's sleeping form, and it wasn't a soft landing either.

"Ooph!" Odelia grunted, when a flying blorange obstacle landed squarely on her stomach. She stared down at me. "Max! Where's the fire?!"

I gave her a sheepish look. "Wakey-wakey."

I directed a scathing look at Brutus, who gave me a grin. "See, Max? I knew you could do it!"

"So then Brutus gave me a boost and that's how I ended up on your stomach," I finished my account of the recent events.

Odelia, who's blond and petite with the most strikingly green eyes, tied the sash of her bathrobe and gave me a worried look. "I better make that appointment with Vena. I knew I should never have put it off."

My eyes widened to the size of saucers, which for us cats is considerable, since our eyes are a lot smaller than a human's eyes to begin with. "Not Vena!"

"Yes, Vena. With everything that's been going on I totally forgot to make a new appointment but it's obvious now that she was right all along." She placed a comforting hand on my head. "You're overweight, Max. Totally overweight, and I've got no one else to blame but myself."

"I'm not overweight. I'm just... big-boned. It runs in the family."

"It's for your own good," she said. "If you don't start dieting again, you'll just get in trouble."

"I won't get in trouble, I promise!" I cried. Anything not

to have to go to Vena, who is just about the vet from hell. For some reason she loves sticking me with needles and suggesting to Odelia that she feed me kibble that tastes like cardboard. The woman is my own personal tormentor.

"It's not your fault," Odelia said as she started down the stairs. "I indulge you. I keep buying those snacks that you like so much and I probably overfeed you, too."

"No, you don't," I said, desperate now. I trotted after her, my paws sounding heavy on the stairs. "I only eat the bare minimum as it is. In fact I'm always hungry."

She paused and listened to the pounding my paws made on the stairs. "You hear that? That's not normal, Max. You're not supposed to walk like that."

"Like what?" I asked, pausing mid-step.

"Like an elephant trampling in the brush."

"I don't sound like an elephant trampling in the brush," I said indignantly, but made an effort to tread a little lighter. Only problem was, it's hard to tread lightly when you're going downhill. Gravity, you know.

"And Vena said that when you get too big it's bad for your heart. Fat tissue builds up around the organ and that's not a good thing."

"My heart is just fine," I promised, tapping my chest. "Healthy as an ox!"

"And you look like one, too," said Brutus. The black cat was right behind me, and obviously enjoying the conversation tremendously.

"I've booked you an appointment, too, by the way, Brutus," said Odelia now.

We'd reached the bottom of the stairs and she walked into the kitchen to start up the coffeemaker. How people can drink that black sludge is beyond me, but then a lot of stuff humans do makes no sense at all. Like putting a perfectly healthy cat on a diet!

"Me!" cried Brutus. "Why me?!"

"Because Chase told me he doesn't remember the last time you went. So it might as well have been never." She frowned. "Though you are neutered, so you must have gone at least once."

A deep blush crept up Brutus's features. At least I think it did. It was hard to be sure with all that dark hair covering his visage. He cut a quick look at Harriet, who pretended she hadn't heard. "I, um—I'm sure that's not possible," he said now.

"That you're neutered or that you didn't go to the vet in years?" Odelia asked deftly, taking a cup and saucer from the cupboard over the sink.

Brutus appeared to be shrinking before my very eyes, a sight I enjoyed a lot, I have to say. "Both," he said curtly, now actively avoiding Harriet's cool gaze.

"Don't worry, Brutus," said Dooley. "We're all neutered. Max is neutered. I am neutered. Even Harriet is neutered. Isn't that right, Harriet?"

"None of your beeswax," Harriet snapped.

"Beeswaxed?" asked Dooley. "I'm pretty sure the right word is neutered."

"Dooley!" Harriet said with a warning glare.

"What? What did I say?"

"Oh, come off it, you guys," said Odelia, crouching down. "It's nothing to be ashamed about. If you weren't neutered I'm sure we'd have a fresh litter every couple of months, and we can't have that now, can we?"

"I don't see why not," Harriet muttered. It was obviously still a sore point.

"Because I can't take care of so many cats," Odelia said softly. "You see that, don't you?"

"Yeah, just do the math," said Dooley. "Three litters a year times eight kittens a litter that's…" He frowned, looking goofy for a moment, then said, "… a heck of a lot of cats!"

"It is," said Odelia. "And I'd just end up having to bring them to the shelter. And I don't need to tell you what happens to cats that end up at the animal shelter, do I?"

"They are adopted by loving humans?" Dooley ventured.

"They die, Dooley," Brutus growled. "They all die."

Dooley uttered a cry of horror and staggered back a few paces. "No, they don't!"

"Oh, yes, they do. And then they're turned into sausages and people eat them!"

"Brutus!" Odelia said. "Don't scare Dooley." She gave Dooley a comforting pat on the back. "They're not turned into sausages. But they're not adopted, either, I'm afraid. At least not all of them. Though I'm sure a lot of them find warm and loving families."

"See!" Dooley cried triumphantly. "They're all placed with their very own Odelias!"

"Thanks," said Odelia, rising to her feet. "Now about Vena…"

Lucky for us the bell rang at that exact moment, and Gran came rushing in through the glass sliding door, looking like she was about to lay an egg.

"Is he here?!" Gran croaked anxiously. "Is he here?!"

"Is who here?" asked Odelia, moving to the front door.

"The UPS guy, of course!"

Gran is a white-haired little old lady, but even though she looks like sweetness incarnate, she's quite a pistol.

"See?" asked Dooley, turning to me. "This is what I told you."

"What did you tell me?" I asked. The morning had already been so traumatizing my mind had actively started to repress the memories.

"About Gran ordering a bunch of stuff online and Marge and Tex having to pay for it."

Odelia had opened the door and Dooley was right: a pimply teenager in a brown uniform with 'UPS' on his chest stood before her, a big, bulky package in his hands. "Vesta Muffin?" he asked.

"That's me!" Gran squealed and darted forward, grabbed the package from the teenager's hands and ran to the living room with it.

Odelia signed for the package and sent the kid on his way. "What's going on, Gran?" she asked.

"Oh, nothing," said Gran, eagerly tearing open the package.

We all gathered around, and since it's hard to see anything from the floor, we all hopped up onto the chairs to have a good look at this mysterious package.

Gran, licking her lips, finally succeeded in ripping away the packaging, and before us lay three shiny green eggs. Huh.

"Gran," said Odelia in her warning voice. It's the voice she likes to use when me or Dooley have been up to no good, which, obviously, practically never happens.

"What?" asked Gran innocently. "I need them. I'm dating again."

What a bunch of green eggs had to do with dating was beyond me, but, like I said, humans are weird. And in my personal experience no human is weirder than Gran.

"You're dating again?" asked Odelia. "I thought that after Leo you were done with all of that."

Leo was a horny old man that Gran used to run around with. We kept bumping into them in the weirdest places, practicing the weirdest positions. All very disturbing.

"Done with dating?" asked Gran indignantly. "Oh, the horror! How can anyone be done with dating? Didn't anyone ever tell you that sex only gets better with age?"

"Like a fine wine," said Dooley, though I doubted he knew what he was talking about.

"The only thing that doesn't improve is my hoo-hee. Which is why I need these."

"What is a hoo-hee?" asked Dooley innocently.

Odelia blushed slightly. "Nothing you should concern yourself with, Dooley."

"You don't know what a hoo-hee is?" asked Gran, raising an eyebrow. "What about hoo-ha? Lady bits? Fine China? Lady garden? Vajayjay?"

Dooley shook his head. "Doesn't ring a bell."

Gran laughed. "You're funny, Dooley. Doesn't ring a bell. I'll bet it doesn't ring your bell, but it sure as heck rung Leo's bell, and there's plenty of Leos out there."

"I'll just bet there are," Odelia muttered, picking up one of the green eggs. "So how do you use these?" Then she noticed four pairs of cat eyes following her every movement and she put the egg down again. "Never mind. I'm sure I don't want to know."

"And I'm sure you do," said Gran. "If you want to entertain your fellow you need to practice the fine art of the jade egg, honey."

"Something to do with energy and healing, right?" asked Odelia with a frown.

Gran threw her head back and laughed. "Of course not! It's all about training those pelvic muscles. You want to get a good grip on your fella's…" She cast a quick look at Dooley. "… fella. Increase the pleasure—his and yours. Trust me," she said as she placed one of the green eggs in the palm of Odelia's hand, "you'll make your man very, very happy."

"That happy, huh?" asked Odelia as she rolled the smooth green egg in her hand.

"Happier," said Gran as she let the other two eggs disappear into the pockets of her dress. She gestured at the box.

"Can you let this disappear, honey? Your mom and dad don't need to know."

"Wait a minute," said Odelia. "You're not going to have this... stuff arrive here from now on, are you?"

"Of course I am. I hate to break it to you, Odelia, but your parents are ageists. They think just because I'm old I'm all shriveled up down there." She patted her granddaughter on the cheek. "Nothing could be further from the truth. In fact I'm pretty sure I get more nookie than those dried-up old prunes."

"Hey, that's my parents you're talking about."

"I know, which is why I'm so glad you're nothing like them. You wouldn't stand in the way of your grandmother enjoying her golden years, would you?"

"No, but..."

"Of course you wouldn't." She gave Odelia a fat wink. "Stick around, kid. You may learn a trick or two from this old dame."

And with these words, she practically galloped through the sliding door and disappeared into the garden, no doubt eager to start practicing those eggs on her hoo-hee, whatever a hoo-hee was.

For a long moment, silence reigned, then Odelia said, "Right. I think I'll just put that egg away, shall I?"

"So what is it for, exactly?" asked Harriet.

Odelia produced an awkward smile. "Decorative purposes?"

Harriet narrowed her eyes at her. "A decorative egg is going to make Chase very, very happy?"

"Yes, it will," Odelia trudged on bravely. "Chase likes a nicely decorated... room."

She was backtracking towards the staircase, and we all watched her go. Then, suddenly, she turned around and popped up the stairs. We heard her rummage around in her bedroom, a drawer opening and closing. Those drawers contained a lot of funny-looking stuff. Amongst other things, they also contained a small battery-powered rocket, though I had no idea why Odelia would need a pocket rocket in her bedroom.

Moments later, she returned, still that sheepish look on her face.

Humans. They're just too weird.

Just then, the doorbell rang again.

"More eggs?" asked Harriet acerbically.

But when Odelia went to open the door, it was her uncle. Chief of Police Alec Lip. Like me, Chief Alec is big-boned. And, also like me, he's a great guy. Always ready with a smile or a kind remark, which makes him real popular with the locals. He wasn't smiling now, though, and when he opened his mouth to speak, it soon became clear why. "There's been a murder. A really nasty one."

CHAPTER 3

*O*delia put the four cats in her old Ford pickup and followed Uncle Alec as he set the course in his police cruiser.

"So who died?" asked Max, who'd crawled up on the passenger seat, as was his habit when there was no one else in the car. No other humans, at least.

"A woman named Donna Bruce," said Odelia, anxiously peering through the windshield. "She's the one who sold Gran those green eggs."

"She's a farmer?" asked Max.

"No, she's not a farmer. She's a former actress who now runs a lifestyle website. A very popular one." She shook her head. "I don't know what's happening in this town. It's just one murder after another. If this keeps up, no tourists are going to want to come here anymore."

"Why did Uncle Alec say it was a nasty murder?" asked Dooley from the backseat.

"Because the woman was murdered in a gruesome way."

She could hear Dooley gulp. Gran's cat was a sensitive plant when it came to things like murder, and she was starting to wonder if it was such a good idea to bring him along. Max, she knew, could handle himself, and so could Brutus and Harriet. But Dooley was the baby of the cat menagerie, and sometimes got spooked by his own shadow. "Maybe you better wait in the car, Dooley," she suggested. "While the others snoop around."

"But I want to snoop around, too," said Dooley. "I love snooping around."

She smiled. That was obvious. All her cats loved snooping around, which was why she took them along in the first place. They often talked to other pets, or even pets that belonged to the victims, and had proved invaluable when ferreting out clues.

Her uncle Alec was aware of this unique talent. Chase? Not so much, though by now he was used to this quirky side of her personality. He even thought it was cute. She'd never told him she could communicate with her cats, though, and probably never would. He might not take it too well.

She thought about Chase and a warm and fuzzy feeling spread through her chest. She'd never thought she would fall for the rugged cop but she had. And by the looks of things, he liked her, too, which was a real boon. They even shared a comfortable working relationship now, which was very different from the way things were when they first met. The burly cop, a recent transplant from the NYPD, wasn't used to nosy reporters investigating a bunch of crimes alongside him. Fortunately she'd quickly proven her worth, and now he was more than happy to allow her to tag along.

As if he'd read her mind, Max asked, "So how are things between you and Chase?"

"Yeah," Harriet chimed in. "When are you going to get married?"

She saw how Max and Dooley shared a quick look of

panic and laughed. "Hold your horses, young lady. Who said anything about me and Chase getting married?"

"It's all over town," said Harriet with a shrug. "All the cats are talking about it."

"Which means all the Hampton Covians are talking about it," Max said.

That was true enough. The Hampton Cove cat community was like a barometer of the human community. She blushed slightly. "So what are they saying, exactly?"

"Well, that the wedding will take place later this year, though it might be sooner rather than later because the first baby is already underway." The gorgeous Persian screwed up her face. "What is a shotgun wedding, Odelia?"

Odelia's blush deepened. "A shotgun wedding? Is that what they're saying?"

All four cats nodded. "I think it means that everybody brings a shotgun to the wedding," said Brutus knowingly.

"Don't be an idiot," said Max. "Why would anyone bring a shotgun to a wedding? That's just dumb."

"Who are you calling dumb, fatso? They're obviously bringing shotguns to make sure nobody crashes the wedding. Duh."

"Crashes the wedding?" asked Dooley. "Is that even a thing?"

"Didn't you see that movie last week? *Wedding crashers*? Two guys go around crashing weddings and having a blast," said Brutus.

"Until they fall in love and get married themselves," said Harriet. "I thought it was the most romantic thing ever. Though I didn't like that they portrayed Bradley Cooper as such a nasty person. I like Bradley Cooper. He's so handsome and cute."

"He's not that handsome," said Brutus. "His mouth is too big for his face."

"It is not. His mouth is just the right size."

"The right size for what?" scoffed Brutus. "To load a Big Mac in one bite?"

"Listen, you guys," said Odelia, interrupting this fascinating discussion of Bradley Cooper's face. "For one thing, Chase and I are not getting married. And for another, I'm not pregnant so there won't be a shotgun wedding."

"That's too bad," said Harriet, her face falling. "I was looking forward to being a bridesmaid."

"That's impossible," said Max. "Cats can't be bridesmaids. That's just preposterous."

Harriet narrowed her eyes. "What are you saying, Max? That I wouldn't make a wonderful bridesmaid? For your information, I would be the perfect bridesmaid. I don't even have to wear a dress. I'm beautiful just the way I am."

Odelia smiled. "That's true. And if I ever get married, you guys will all get to come."

Max groaned. "Do I have to? I hate weddings. Everybody is always crying. Those things are even worse than funerals."

"People are crying because they're happy, Max," said Odelia. "Those are happy tears."

"I don't get it," said the blorange cat. "Why cry when you're happy? That doesn't make sense."

"Yes, it does," said Harriet. "You wouldn't understand, though, Max. And that's because you're a Neanderthal."

"No, I'm not," said Max. "I'm a cat, not a Neanderthal."

"What's a Neanderthal?" asked Dooley.

"It's a kind of old human," said Max. "With a lot of hair and a big mouth."

"Like Bradley Cooper," said Brutus.

"Bradley Cooper is not a Neanderthal!" Harriet snapped. "Bradley Cooper is gorgeous."

"More gorgeous than me?" asked Brutus, stung.

Harriet's face softened. "Of course not, cutie pie. Nobody can be more gorgeous than you."

"Maybe *you* should have one of those shotgun weddings," Max grumbled. "So I can bring a shotgun and shoot myself."

"We're here," said Odelia cheerfully, cutting off all this nonsense about a shotgun wedding. She just hoped those rumors hadn't reached her mother's ears. Nobody likes to hear about their daughter's supposed pregnancy and forced wedding because of gossip. Then again, maybe it was a good thing. If people thought she and Chase were about to get married, she should probably take it as a compliment. Though the town's gossip mill was obviously getting a little ahead of itself this time around.

True, there had been a lot of kissing lately, but things hadn't progressed beyond that. Yet. Did she want them to go beyond that stage? Maybe. Did Chase want to? She had absolutely no idea. Chase was one of those strong, silent types. The ones that don't wear their hearts on their sleeves. Beyond those kisses they had yet to address whatever it was that was going on between them. Heck, he hadn't even asked her out. Maybe he never would? Maybe those kisses were just a way of showing his appreciation for all she'd done for the community? Maybe it was an NYPD thing: instead of shaking hands, NYPD cops simply kissed their colleagues. It was definitely not something she'd ever seen on *NYPD Blue*. Then again, they never showed everything on those shows.

She parked right behind her uncle's squad car and got out, allowing the four cats to jump from their respective seats.

"Let's go, guys," she said. "You know the drill. Talk to witnesses. Try to find out what happened here."

She watched the cats traipse up to the house and smiled. Her own personal feline detective squad. She wouldn't know what to do without them.

She watched her uncle take off his sunglasses and take in their surroundings. Donna Bruce had done well for herself, that much was obvious. The house was built in hacienda style, with a low red-tile roof and stuccoed orange outer walls.

"Nice place," said Uncle Alec admiringly. "Though more like something one would expect in the Hollywood Hills than out here in Hampton Cove."

"Isn't Donna originally from Los Angeles?"

"She is. She only moved out here to put some distance between herself and her ex-husband. And because her company is headquartered in New York."

"This is such a coincidence," Odelia said as she watched the police activity around the house. Half a dozen squad cars were haphazardly parked on the circular driveway, and an ambulance stood, lights flashing, indicating the coroner was already there.

"What is?" asked her uncle, hoisting his pants over his bulk and patting down his few strands of hair.

"Just this morning a package arrived from donna.vip for your mother."

Chief Alec closed his eyes. "God, not again. I thought Marge put a stop to that nonsense."

"What nonsense?"

"Didn't she tell you? Your grandmother has been ordering those packages for weeks now. She's addicted to that Donna crap. And the worst part? Your mom has been footing the bill as Vesta doesn't have a credit card. Marge told me she's up to five grand now."

Odelia's jaw dropped. "Five grand!"

"Yeah, for a bunch of useless stuff. According to Marge she even bought one of those steamers for her, um, well, you know what."

Odelia frowned. "A vegetable steamer?"

Uncle Alec suddenly looked uncomfortable. "Not exactly. She uses it on her… business."

"Her business?"

He heaved an exasperated groan. "Her lady parts, all right?"

Odelia smiled. "She bought a vaginal steamer?" Uncle Alec grumbled something under his breath as he stalked off. She hurried to keep up with him. "No wonder Mom is mad. That stuff must cost a fortune."

"And it's not as if she needs it," said her uncle. "I mean, she's seventy-five, for crying out loud. What does she need a vaginal steamer for?"

"Well, she does have a very active sex life."

Uncle Alec winced. He directed a pleading look at his niece. "Please, Odelia. I don't need to hear all that."

Which was probably why Mom had allowed this buying frenzy to go on as long as it had. Nobody wanted to sit down with Gran and have a serious conversation about her sex life. It wasn't a topic one simply launched into.

"I'll talk to Gran," she promised. "Tell her to ease up on the spending."

"You do that," her uncle grumbled.

They walked into the house and Odelia admired her surroundings. Donna Bruce had taste, that much was obvious. The foyer had a homey feel, with its hardwood floors, soft pink wallpaper and white lacquered furniture. And as they progressed into the living room and then the kitchen, she had to admit she wouldn't mind living in a place like this. Selling jade eggs and vaginal steamers had obviously been very lucrative for the founder of donna.vip.

They reached the spa area, where a small indoor pool awaited them, along with the sauna cabin where Donna's housekeeper had found the body of her employer that morning.

"You better prepare yourself for a shock," said Uncle Alec. "It's not a pretty sight."

She braced herself and stepped into the sauna. Donna Bruce was lying on the floor, partly covered by a towel, her face swollen beyond recognition. Every part of her body that was visible had suffered the same fate. The woman had literally been stung to death.

She swallowed. "How—how did they get the bees in here?"

Uncle Alec gestured at the fan that was placed in the ceiling. "They reversed the airflow and placed an entire batch of bees on top of it. The little beasties must have been pretty pissed off when they were propelled past the fan's blades and into this extremely hot environment. They simply attacked the first thing they came into contact with. Which was Donna Bruce."

"I'm guessing she died from anaphylactic shock," said the coroner, who was standing in a corner, picking up the body of a dead bee and dumping it into a plastic baggie. Abe Cornwall was a shabbily-dressed man with frizzy gray hair but he was an ace medical examiner. "Though judging from the state of the body, she might have died from the venom itself. She must have sustained thousands of stings in a matter of minutes."

"This entire cabin was full of bees when the housekeeper arrived," Uncle Alec explained. "Thousands and thousands of them."

"And there's no question whether this was an accident or not?" asked Odelia.

"No way," another male voice spoke.

She turned around with a smile, and got a small shock of pleasure when she found herself gazing into the gold-flecked chocolate eyes of Chase Kingsley. He filled the entire doorframe with his muscular physique, and the cabin with his powerful presence. "So it was definitely murder, huh?"

"Definitely," said Chase with a smile of greeting.

"I'll let you two kids come up with a theory as to who's responsible," said Uncle Alec. "I have to talk to the ex-husband about what to do with the kids."

"The kids?" asked Odelia.

"Yeah." Uncle Alec frowned at his notebook. "Sweetums and Honeychild. Good thing they weren't here when it happened."

"Oh, those poor babies," said Odelia.

"Big babies," said Uncle Alec. "Sweetums and Honeychild are six." He shook his head. "Who gives their kid a name like that?"

"Donna Bruce," said Chase, staring down at the victim. He glanced up at the chief. "So am I in charge of this thing, Chief?"

"Yes, you are," said Chief Alec. "Along with Odelia—in an entirely unofficial capacity, of course."

Chase gave her a grin. "Looks like the gang is back together, babe."

She returned his smile. "Yay."

CHAPTER 4

"*D*o you really think Odelia is getting married?" asked Dooley.

I shook my head. "No way. Odelia doesn't lie. If she was getting married she would have told us. In fact I'm pretty sure we'd be the first to know."

"But why is everybody saying she's having this shotgun wedding?"

"People talk, Dooley. You know that and I know that. That's what they do."

He thought about this for a moment. "You know, you might be right, Max."

"Of course I'm right. I'm always right. You should know that by now."

We were walking around the back of the house. I don't know what we were hoping to find, but at least something that would shed some light on what had happened here. And if we were really lucky, maybe even an eyewitness account of the murder with a nice description of the murderer. Humans might think they're pretty smart by avoiding the attention of other humans when they're out murdering each other, but they never give a second thought to the pets they encounter along the way.

Behind us, Harriet and Brutus were still engaged in their lover's quarrel.

"I don't see why you have to go and fall for this Bradley Cooper guy," Brutus was saying. "Not only does he have the face of a Neanderthal but he's human! Cats don't fall for humans. That's not natural, Harriet. And it's humiliating for me as your boyfriend."

"I just like his face," said Harriet. "Is that so bad? He has a fascinating face."

"A human face," Brutus pointed out. "You can't like a human face, sweet pea."

"I can, too. You can't tell me what I can and can't like, Brutus. I'm a free cat."

"Oh, is that why you were kissing Max the other day? Huh?"

She rolled her eyes. "Oh, God. Not again! I wasn't kissing Max. I already told you what happened."

"Yeah, you stubbed your toe and you tripped and fell and ended up hitting Max's lips with yours. I know what you told me. I'm just telling you I'm not buying it. Who trips and hits another cat's lips? That's just crazy! Besides, why did you keep on kissing him for a full minute after that?"

She heaved an exasperated groan. "Like I said this morning, I thought he was you, sugar lump. Until I discovered he wasn't and then I stopped."

Brutus shook his head. "I don't know, bunny duck. I just don't know."

"Oh, buttercup," she said, taking his head in her paws. "You know I only love you. My very own cuddly daddy."

At this, Brutus seemed to relent, his scowl melting away like butter on the griddle. "Oh, my snookums," he purred. "Sweetie cakes."

"Chocolate bunny."

"Smoochie poo."

And then, inevitably, there was smooching. A lot of smooching.

Dooley moaned. "Why do they have to do that right under our noses?!"

"Because they only have eyes for each other, Dooley," I said. "Wait until you're in love."

"I'm never falling in love again," said Dooley bitterly. "Love is a curse."

We managed to put some distance between ourselves and the loved-up couple, and a good thing, too. Brutus has this competitive streak. Whenever there is a murder to solve, he wants to solve it first, and he doesn't care what he has to do to 'win.'

We'd arrived in the backyard and I raised an eyebrow in admiration. The yard was perfectly maintained, the grass as smooth as a pool table. An actual pool had been installed, with an actual pool house and a nice row of chaise lounges placed right next to it. It all looked very inviting, or it would have if Dooley and I were human. As it was I didn't care about pools. Not that I'm scared of pools. I just don't like that they're full of water. Water is wet.

And that's when I saw them: two poodles, one brown, one beige, were lying on top of the chaise lounges, their eyes closed, enjoying some R&R.

"I think we might have our first witnesses," I told Dooley, gesturing with my head to the two mutts.

"Dogs?" asked Dooley. "Why does it always have to be dogs? Why can't rich people keep cats instead?"

"Because they think dogs are great for keeping the burglars away."

"Cats keep burglars away," Dooley argued. "In fact we're better equipped for the task. We can see in the dark. Dogs can't. And we have sharp claws. Dogs have those silly excuses for claws."

"Dogs can bite," I reminded him. "And they bark."

"I meow! Have you heard my meow? I meow up a storm."

"Not exactly the same, Dooley."

The dogs had spotted us and had curled their upper lips up in a snarl, making that annoying threatening noise at the back of their throats. As if that was supposed to impress us. Puh-lease.

"Hey there, guys," I said, walking up to the duo. "How's it hanging?"

"And who are you?" asked the brown poodle, none too friendly.

"My name is Max," I said by way of introduction. "You may have heard of me. I'm an ace feline detective. And I'm here to solve the murder."

"Murder? What murder?" asked the beige one.

"The murder of your human? Don't tell me no one told you."

"Our human wasn't murdered," said the brown one. "She's just sleeping. In the sauna. Isn't that right, Rex?"

"That's right, Rollo. She's just taking a little nap in the sauna. I just saw her."

"And I saw her, too."

"She's not sleeping," said Dooley, venturing up with some trepidation. "She's dead."

Rex and Rollo shared a look of amusement, then burst out laughing. "No, she's not," said Rex. "You silly cat. You're funny. Hasn't anyone ever told you that humans have to sleep just like we do?"

"Yeah, and when they sleep they look dead but they aren't," Rollo added.

"Look, I've had a human since forever," I said. "So you don't have to teach me the difference between a dead human and a sleeping human. I know the difference. One is breathing and the other ain't. And for your information, your human isn't sleeping—she's dead."

"Cats," said Rex, shaking his head. "They're a real hoot."

"Yeah. Think they know it all."

They placed their chins on their front paws again and stared at us, quickly losing interest.

"So tell me why there are so many cops around?" I said, not giving up.

Rex shrugged. "Donna likes to invite people."

"Yeah, Donna's a real people person. Always hosting parties."

"For the police?" I asked.

"Sure," said Rollo. "Why not? Police are human, too. They like to party."

"Only they're not partying now, are they?" I asked, exasperated. "They're examining the dead body of your human, trying to figure out who made her that way."

Rex and Rollo shared another knowing look, then shook their heads with a smirk. "Cats," Rollo repeated. "You gotta love them."

"What about the ambulance parked out in front of the house?" Dooley asked.

"Oh, please," said Rollo, rolling his eyes. "When you have a party, you have to have an ambulance. In case one of the guests suddenly gets sick."

"Remember that party where all the guests got sick, Rollo?" asked Rex. "Remember that? That was some party."

"We don't mention that," said Rollo sternly. "We never mention that party, Rex. That party never happened."

"Oh. Right. Totally forgot about that."

Rollo eyed us critically. "There was never any party where everybody got sick after eating the shrimp. And Donna never sued the caterer. Is that understood, cats?"

"My name is Max," I reminded him.

"Whatever, cat," said Rollo. "Now I think you better scram. I don't remember seeing your name on the guest list. And if Donna finds out you're trespassing and we're allowing you, she'll have something to say about it."

"Oh, you think we should chase them off the premises, Rollo?" asked Rex.

Rollo thought about this for a moment. "Maybe we'll just let them off with a warning this time."

"Great," said Rex with a smile. "I'm not in the mood for running around anyway."

"Come on, you guys!" I said. "Your human is dead! You have to snap out of it and help us catch the killer!"

Rollo's face clouded. "On second thought..."

"Uh-oh," Dooley muttered.

Rollo turned to Rex. "Rex. You get the fat one. I'll get the skinny one. Go!"

Good thing for us the dogs had more bark than bite. And more talk than dash. By the time Dooley and I had cleared the pool area, they were still nowhere near catching up with us.

"See?" asked Dooley, slightly out of breath as we hid under Odelia's pickup. "That's another advantage us cats have over dogs: we're a lot faster!"

Or these two idiots were exceptionally slow, I thought as I saw Rex and Rollo appear around the corner and search around stupidly. Then, in perfect unison, they both plunked down on their haunches and started licking their private parts.

"Yuck," Dooley muttered. "Imagine being the tongue of a dog. Just... yuck."

"You lick your private parts," I reminded him.

"Yeah, but I'm a cat. I'm naturally clean. Dogs are just filthy."

He had a point, of course. Dogs *are* filthy, and cats *are* naturally clean.

"So now what?" I asked. "Our only potential witnesses are two dumb-ass dogs."

"With the emphasis on ass," said Dooley as he watched Rex and Rollo turn their attention from their private parts to a different, even filthier part of their canine anatomy.

"Let's just hope Brutus and Harriet have better luck," I said.

Just then, Brutus and Harriet emerged from inside the house. They were still gabbing away, probably discussing Bradley Cooper's face and why it was off limits to cats. Rex and Rollo paused from their hygienic pursuit to gawk at the two newcomers.

"Uh-oh," said Dooley. "Here we go."

Within seconds, Brutus and Harriet had joined us underneath the car, scared off by those two idiot poodles, who were now sniffing around in the vicinity of the boxwood hedge.

"So? What did you find out?" I asked.

"That Bradley Cooper is the only human who looks good with a beard," Brutus said morosely.

"Well, he does!" Harriet cried. "That man makes a beard look totally sexy."

"Because it hides his big mouth!"

"It does not!"

Brutus, Dooley and I shared an agonized groan. "What about the murder?" I asked.

"What about it?" asked Harriet.

"Did you talk to anyone inside? Did Donna Bruce have other pets besides Beavis and Butt-head over there?"

Dooley snickered. "You said butt."

"For your information, that place is filled with cops," said

Harriet. "So even if there were any pets around, the cops probably scared them off."

Now it was my turn to place my chin on my front paws. This investigation was not exactly going the way I'd hoped. "So nothing?" I asked.

Harriet remained conspicuously silent.

"At least now we know that Bradley Cooper looks great with a beard," Dooley offered. "That's something, right? Right, Max?"

"Oh, Dooley," I muttered.

CHAPTER 5

*I*nside the house, Odelia and Chase sat down with Hillary Davies, who was the CEO of donna.vip. Hillary, a fortysomething woman with short blond hair streaked with gray and a square face, knitted her brows. "I still can't believe Donna's dead. That's just not like her."

Odelia would have said it wasn't like anyone to be dead, but she thought she understood. Donna Bruce had apparently been one of those extremely dynamic women, possessing a very strong personality and an iron will to succeed. People like that often seemed indestructible.

She handed the CEO a cup of chamomile tea. Hillary took it gratefully, the cup shaking between her fingers as she put it to her lips.

"How long have you known Donna Bruce?" Odelia asked.

"I started to work for her five years ago, so that's when our relationship began, though I was a customer way before that. Donna.vip was already an established brand by that time, and Donna felt that in order to expand, she needed to professionalize and hire a CEO. And that's where I came in."

"Was she tough to work for?" asked Odelia.

Hillary smiled. "She wasn't easy to work for, that's for sure. She was demanding and outspoken. And she definitely didn't keep her opinions to herself. But she was also generous and eager to give credit where credit was due. She lived for the brand, so if you improved the brand, she considered you a friend."

"And did you? Improve the brand?" asked Chase.

"Yes, I think I did," said the woman, tilting her chin. "I took it from twenty million annual gross to two hundred, and I like to believe I played a big part in that expansion. And judging from the bonus Donna paid me last Christmas, I think she knew it too."

"Did she have any enemies?" Odelia asked.

"Oh, more than I can count on the fingers of my two hands," said Hillary. "A strong and visible woman like Donna Bruce will always rub a lot of people the wrong way and she was no exception."

"Can you think of anyone who could have killed her?" asked Chase.

Hillary thought for a moment, touching her lips with her fingers. "Well, there was her ex-husband, of course."

"Tad Rip," Chase read from his notes.

"That's right. He didn't like it when Donna got sole custody of Sweetums and Honeychild. And he certainly didn't like it when she called him a drug addict, a drunk and a serial philanderer. Claimed it ruined his reputation."

"What does he do, this ex-husband?" asked Odelia.

"He's one of those Silicon Valley tycoons," said Hillary. "You know the type. Multi-millionaire before the age of twelve and an ego bigger than the state of Alaska. The man was a buffoon, plain and simple, and spent more time bedding his secretaries than trying to make his marriage work." She leaned forward. "In my opinion the only reason he married Donna was so he could leverage her success to his advantage. A trophy wife on steroids. But Donna wasn't having it and he paid the price."

"So you think he might have murdered the mother of his own children?" asked Odelia, surprised.

Hillary pressed her lips together. "You didn't hear it from me, but the man is a sociopath. Which I guess is a quality that comes in handy when you're trying to make it to the top of the heap in Silicon Valley."

Chase smiled. "Sounds to me like you're not a big fan of Mr. Rip."

"No, I'm not. The man tried to damage our business, claiming donna.vip was just a silly little whim. Around the time of the divorce there was a hostile takeover attempt I'm sure was instigated by Mr. Rip. Luckily with the help of a few private backers we managed to get it overturned. It's clear to me Donna's ex tried to destroy her company out of sheer spite."

"And now he's destroyed its owner and founder," Odelia said softly.

"As I said, you didn't hear it from me. I'm still the CEO, and it's a tough world out there. I don't need this to come back to me."

"What do you think will happen to the company now that Donna is gone?" Chase asked.

"I have no idea. I just hope she made the necessary arrangements. Many of these business tycoons don't, thinking they're immortal. And then when they die the whole thing is taken over by a bunch of bumbling relatives and run into the ground within a year. I hope she didn't make that mistake."

They left Hillary to take an urgent business call, and

ambled into the kitchen, where the housekeeper, Jackie Laboeuf, was busy preparing breakfast. The sturdily-built woman with the raven-black hair looked up when they entered.

"Hi, Mrs. Laboeuf," said Chase, producing his badge. "My name is Chase Kingsley and I'm the detective in charge of this case. This is Odelia Poole, civilian consultant to the Hampton Cove Police Department. Can we ask you a few questions?"

The woman sniffed, dabbing a handkerchief the size of a dish towel to her eyes. "Ask away, Detective. The sooner you catch the monster that did this the better. How anyone could hurt Mrs. B is beyond me. The woman was a saint."

"You were the one who found her?"

"Yes, I'm sorry to say that I was. I come in every morning around eight, to take care of breakfast and organize the household, and usually when I arrive Mrs. B is waiting for me and we sit down to discuss any ongoing things and plan out the rest of the day. But this morning as I let myself in with my key there was no one here. And when I went looking for her, I…" Her voice faltered and she brought the dish towel to her eyes again, then proceeded to loudly blow her nose in it. "I'm sorry. This has all come as a big shock to me."

"Wasn't there any security?" asked Odelia.

Jackie shook her head. "Mrs. B fired See-Cure last week. They weren't up to her usual standards. There had been reporters that had managed to get close to the house, with one even snapping a picture of Mrs. B while she was taking a bath. You may have seen the picture. It was all over the Internet."

"So she fired the security company but didn't replace them?"

"She was in talks with one other company operating out of Amagansett, but the contracts hadn't been signed yet, so the cameras were all switched off and the fence wasn't hooked up to anything. But we did have the dogs, so Mrs. B wasn't worried."

"Right," said Chase dubiously. "Rex and Rollo. Not exactly guard dogs, are they?"

"They're pretty good barkers. And they'll bite anyone they don't like, especially reporters."

It was obvious the housekeeper wasn't fond of reporters, which wasn't surprising as they hadn't been kind to Donna Bruce and her website, heaping more scorn on her and her project than praise over the years.

"Do you have any idea who might have done this to her?" asked Odelia.

Jackie Laboeuf shook her head, tears springing to her eyes again. "It might be those reporters," she said, harping on the same theme.

"But why would a reporter murder Donna Bruce?" asked Chase.

"They hated her," the housekeeper burst out. "For some reason they just hated her. And is it so hard to believe that one of them just went nuts and killed her? That lot is obviously capable of anything."

"What about Mrs. Bruce's ex-husband?" asked Odelia. "Tad Rip?"

Jackie shrugged. "It might have been him. Though why he would kill the mother of his children is beyond me. He might be a douche but he's not a murdering douche."

"So you knew Mr. Rip?"

"Of course I knew Mr. Rip. I've been working for Mrs. B for coming up on fifteen years now," she said proudly. "I was here when they brought Sweetums and Honeychild home.

Such a happy couple they were back then. You should have seen how proud Mr. Rip was. But that was before he and Mrs. B had a falling-out, of course."

"Why did they divorce?" asked Odelia.

"Couldn't keep his hands off his secretaries," said Jackie with a snort. "She forgave him more than once, but after the fifth or the sixth—I lost count—she kicked him out. Even made sure he never got to see his kids again." She shook her head. "That was one mean divorce. All fought out in the press, of course."

"Of course," said Odelia softly. "What's going to happen to the kids now?"

"They'll go and live with their father I suppose," said Jackie. Then, as the uncertainty of her own fate came home to her, she dissolved into tears again.

When they left the unfortunate housekeeper, she'd just taken out a clean dish towel and was burying her face in it.

"So sad," Odelia murmured as they stepped into the foyer.

"Yeah, the poor woman was obviously very attached to her employer," Chase agreed. "Which doesn't mean we should rule her out as a suspect, of course."

"A suspect? But why? Why would she kill Donna? She's not only losing her position but obviously one she was extremely fond of."

"I don't know," said Chase, fiddling with his notebook. "That's what we're here to find out."

There was a commotion outside, and Odelia looked up. The ruckus seemed to come from the front gate, and when they stepped outside, she saw that a group of protesters were marching down the drive in the direction of the house. A few of the police officers tried to head them off, and the end result was a very voluble confrontation.

"Who are those people?" she asked as she watched the scene.

"Let's find out, shall we?" Chase suggested, and set foot for the altercation.

She followed him reluctantly. She hadn't come here to get into a brawl with a bunch of protestors. When they came closer, she saw that they were brandishing placards that read, 'Down With The Wall!' 'No To The Wall!' 'Don't Take Away Our Sun!'

"What's all this?" asked Chase as he addressed what appeared to be the most vocal protestor of the bunch. He was a red-haired red-faced man shouting, 'Down With The Wall!' at the top of his lungs, while engaged in a shoving match with two officers.

"They want to have a word with Donna Bruce, sir," said one of the officers.

"You damn right we want to have a word with Donna Bruce!" the protestor yelled. "She will build her wall over our dead bodies! Do you hear me, cop! Over my dead body!"

He'd gotten right in Chase's face. Spittle was flying and testosterone was pumping.

"I need you to back off, sir," said Chase. "This is private property."

"I don't care!" yelled the guy. "I want to see Donna and I'm not leaving until I do!"

"I'm afraid that's not possible," said Chase, his face reddening.

"And who's going to stop me, huh? You? You're all protecting her, aren't you? The whole lot of you! Well, I'm not taking any more of this crap!"

And with these words, he charged forward, embarking on a mad dash toward the house. But he hadn't counted on Chase, who uttered a few choice curse words and then chased after the man, tackling him before he'd gone twenty yards.

The protestor, obviously not too well pleased, screamed,

"Get off me, you Nazi pig!" and proceeded to hit Chase over the head with his placard. At this, Chase hauled off and hit the man in the eye. "Hey! What did you have to go and do that for?!" said the protestor dumbly, and then promptly collapsed on the ground, out for the count.

CHAPTER 6

*T*he reenactment of *Fight Club* had taken us by surprise. Hidden beneath Odelia's pickup, we'd had a first-row seat to the entire show, from the arrival of the dozen or so protestors to the takedown of the most fiery one of the lot by Chase. The man soon came to, and was tucked into a squad car and shipped off to the police station.

"Wow, did you see that?" asked Brutus. "That was one great punch!"

"Such a violent man," tsk-tsked Harriet.

"Yeah, good thing Chase was here to take him out," I said.

"I mean Chase. Who goes and punches an innocent man like that?"

We all stared at the Persian. "Wait, what?" I cried. "Chase is the hero here. Who knows what that dude was up to."

"All he was doing was exercising his right to protest as stated in the Constitution."

"Right to protest? He was charging the house!"

"With a placard as a weapon," said Harriet. "Big threat."

"Well, he still had no right to be here. This is private property and he was trespassing."

"*We* are trespassing on private property," Harriet argued. "Nobody ever gave us permission to be here, so technically we're in violation too. But you don't see Chase punching our lights out, do you?"

"That's because we're here with Odelia," I pointed out. "So we're not trespassing at all. We're part of the police effort to find the killer of the owner of this private property."

Harriet studied her nails. "You can argue all you want, Max, but the fact remains that Chase just punched a man and now I'm seeing him in an entirely different light."

"In a great, wonderful light," I said. "In the light of heroism! He saved us from crazy protestor guy."

"The man has a violent streak and I for one think Odelia should be warned."

"He does *not* have a violent streak! He was protecting us!"

"From a placard," said Harriet skeptically.

"I think Harriet is right," said Dooley.

I wheeled around. "What?!"

"Chase had no reason to punch that man. He could have simply pointed out to him in a firm voice that he was trespassing and kindly have requested him to leave."

"He did! And the guy called him a Nazi pig!"

"Well, I'm sure it's all one big misunderstanding," said Dooley vaguely, directing a keen look at Harriet. Then it dawned on me. He was simply trying to get in good with the feisty white cat. Nice! My best friend was openly disagreeing with me so he could score points with Harriet. Great going, Dooley.

Just then, Odelia approached, glanced around, and then whispered, "Max! Dooley! Where are you guys?"

It was our cue and we emerged from beneath the vehicle, but not before taking a look around to ascertain whether Rex and Rollo were gone. They were.

"What were you all doing underneath the car?" asked Odelia with an expression of surprise on her face.

"Oh, just holding an emergency meeting," I said. "Us cats like to hold our meetings under cars. It seems to stimulate our creativity for some reason."

"Yeah, must be the presence of all that oil and grease," said Brutus a little pompously. "Oils the creative processes, it does."

Dooley was rubbing his shoulder where Brutus had just punched him. The big cat had taken a dim view of Dooley's efforts to get in good with his girlfriend and had shown him what he felt about that. As a consequence, Harriet was seeing her beau in an entirely new light as well, for she said, "Why did you punch Dooley, Brutus? That was uncalled for and absolutely unnecessary."

"I, um…" the black cat began.

"You're just as bad as Chase Kingsley," Harriet said with a shake of the head, and then hopped into the pickup, following Odelia's example.

We all filed in after her. "Who was that man Chase knocked out?" asked Harriet.

"Oh, just some protestor," said Odelia, buckling up. She turned to us. "So? What did you guys find out?"

"That Donna Bruce had a very bad taste in pets," I said, and told her about our unproductive encounter with Rex and Rollo.

"And that Chase Kingsley is a very violent man," said Harriet primly.

"And that Bradley Cooper looks great with a beard," Dooley added, earning himself a smile from Harriet and a scowl from Brutus.

Ignoring the remark about Bradley Cooper, Odelia asked, "Why do you think Chase is a violent man, Harriet?"

"Did you not see how he simply knocked out an innocent

bystander, absolutely unprovoked? I think it raises all kinds of issues, Odelia. One of which is that the man is obviously completely out of control."

"I think you've got that wrong, Harriet," said Odelia to my surprise. "Chase was hit over the head by the man. All he did was retaliate."

"See?" I asked triumphantly. "Chase had every right to knock that guy's block off."

"I still think it was uncalled for and very, very rude," Harriet insisted. "And it shows a side of the man's character that I'd never seen before."

"I think it was heroic," I said. "He obviously was trying to protect Odelia."

"Who was in no danger whatsoever," Harriet countered.

"She was. The man is a menace. Someone had to take him down and Chase did."

"I think Harriet is right," Dooley piped up, gulping slightly when Brutus gave him one of his trademark scowls again. "And it's all in the Constitution and all that..." His voice died away.

Odelia, clearly not in the mood for this conversation, said, "Look, I need you to focus on finding Donna Bruce's killer, not comment on Chase's alleged violent tendencies. Are you going to help me or not? If not, that's fine with me. I'll just drop you off at the house and you can continue this pointless discussion indefinitely."

"Oh, no, we are going to help you," I said quickly. "I mean, I am going to help you."

"Me, too," said Brutus. "In fact I'm pretty sure I already know who the killer is. I just need some time to come up with the evidence that will tie this case together."

I eyed him dubiously. I was pretty sure he had no clue who the killer was.

"And I also have a pretty good idea who did it," said Harriet primly.

"Me too," Dooley said weakly. "I'm sure I have a great idea who killed…"

"Donna Bruce," I said helpfully.

"Exactly," Dooley said.

Odelia eyed us with a glint of humor in her eye. "So you all know who the killer is, huh? So when are you going to tell me?" We all started talking simultaneously, and she held up her hands in a bid to silence us. "You need to work together on this, you guys."

"I cannot in all good conscience collaborate with anyone who condones violence," said Harriet, directing a critical eye at me and Brutus. "That is simply out of the question."

"Me either," said Dooley. "I don't violently condone a conscience. Absolutely not."

"Right," said Odelia with a slight grin. "Looks like the allegiances have shifted again. So what I'll do is appoint a lead investigator in this case. He or she will be the one who takes the lead and who will bring this case to a close."

I frowned. What was she talking about? I was her main cat. Always had been. She was my human, after all. Harriet belonged to Marge. Dooley belonged to Vesta. Brutus belonged to Chase. I was the only one who belonged to her. So technically I was the only lead investigator in any case she was involved in. But she ignored my studious frown.

"And I'm picking Harriet," she finally said after a moment's deliberation.

Dooley, Brutus and I all exclaimed "What?!!!"

"Yes, I think Harriet is going to be great," said Odelia with a smile.

Harriet was beaming. "Oh, Odelia, you won't regret this!" she exclaimed. "I'm going to catch this killer for you!"

"I know you will, honey," said Odelia. "The rest of you

guys can just sit this one out, all right? Harriet is going to catch this killer all by herself." And with these words, she turned to the front again and started up the car. It rumbled to life with a throaty purr.

Harriet's smile waned a little. "Wait, what?"

"You're on your own, honey," said Odelia. "Max, Dooley and Brutus are out."

"But…" Harriet frowned, thinking this through. "You mean I have to do this all by myself?"

Odelia glanced over her shoulder. "Is that a problem?"

"No!" Harriet was quick to say. "No, I—I can do this. Of course I can."

"That's what I thought. In fact, now that I come to think of it, Chase and I will sit this one out as well. Chase is entirely too violent—you got that right. And I don't have a clue what I'm doing, as usual." She sighed. "So I guess it's all up to you, honey."

Harriet's lips moved wordlessly, as panic was clear in her eyes. "All up to me," she echoed.

"Yep. Good thing you're up to the task, or else I'd be worried if I was one of Donna Bruce's relatives. Or, God forbid, Sweetums or Honeychild. I'm sure they want to know what happened to their mother, poor kids."

The distinct look of panic in Harriet's eyes had increased. Then, suddenly, she cried out, "Don't do it!"

Odelia frowned. "Don't do what, honey?"

"Don't let me do this by myself! I'm—I'm not up to the task! I—I wouldn't know where to begin. Let's…" She directed a pleading glance in my direction. "Let's all do this together. As a team. Just the way we always do. Please, Odelia?"

Odelia thought about this for a moment. "But I thought you said Brutus was entirely too violent? And so was Max? And, for that matter, Chase? I got the distinct impression you thought you could handle this all on your own, without any help from anyone?"

"No, I can't! I'm sorry! I was just—I was just—I don't know what I was thinking! All I know is that I can't do this without you guys. Brutus—Dooley—Max. We're a team, right? We make a great team."

Odelia smiled. "I'm glad you think so, Harriet. So... are you sure you don't want to do this all by yourself?"

"No, I don't!"

Odelia shrugged. "Okay, then. I guess we're all on board again."

"Yay!" Harriet squealed, doing a happy dance on the backseat.

Odelia locked eyes with me and gave me a wink. I returned it with relish.

My human, people. She's the greatest.

"So from now on Harriet is in charge. You will all follow her lead," Odelia said, and drove off.

My human. She's completely nuts!

CHAPTER 7

*A*fter dropping off the cats at the house, Odelia headed for the police station, to assist Chase while he interviewed the man they'd arrested outside the Donna Bruce residence. Judging from his behavior he was now the prime suspect in the murder of the celebrity lifestyle guru.

She parked in front of the station house and got out. There were a bunch of reporters camped out in front of the squat building, and she wondered if this was going to pose a problem for the investigation. When celebrities were murdered, the accompanying attention sometimes worked disruptive, pushing the people in charge of the investigation to make rash decisions they wouldn't otherwise make. Then again, this was Chase Kingsley. He wasn't the kind of guy to allow emotion to trump reason.

She hiked her purse up her shoulder and headed inside, keeping her head down as the reporters studied her curiously, probably wondering if and how she was connected to the case. Fortunately for her, she had one of those unremarkable faces that easily get lost in the crowd, so they quickly dismissed her and went about their business of interviewing each other on camera.

She waved a greeting at Dolores, the big-haired receptionist manning the front desk, and made her way to her uncle's office at the end of the hallway. When she swept inside, Chase was pacing the room, looking slightly agitated, while her uncle was seated at his desk, his feet up, hands behind his head, the picture of calm and poise.

"I'm telling you, Chief, this is our guy. He's obviously bearing a grudge, he was at the scene, and he is as hostile and aggressive as they come. Now all we have to do is establish means and opportunity and we're home free. Oh, hey, Odelia. We were just discussing the arrest of Alpin Carré."

"The guy who hit you over the head with his placard."

Chase's jaw worked. "That's the one."

She took a seat in front of her uncle. "So you think he might be our guy?"

"I'm ninety-five percent positive."

"And I'm not," said Uncle Alec. "I know Alpin, Chase. He might be a hothead but he's not a killer. Heck, the guy is a publisher. And a very successful one at that. Publishes these books about angels and the healing power of crystals and stuff like that."

"Healing power of crystals? "

"Yeah, he had a real bestseller last year with *The Shed*. I don't know if you've heard about it. Everybody was reading it."

"The book about the guy who finds God while sitting alone in his shed?"

Uncle Alec nodded. "They're turning it into a movie starring Chris Pratt. I think they tapped George Clooney to play the voice of God."

"Great choice," said Odelia. If God had a voice it would be Clooney's. Though in this day and age of gender equality and feminism, maybe Meryl Streep was the more politically correct option.

Chase made a slashing motion with his hand. "Look, I don't care if the guy can walk on water. He's clearly unhinged, so in my book he's our prime suspect."

"What about the ex-husband?" asked Odelia. "Hillary Davies seemed pretty sure he was the one." She turned to her uncle. "Is he in town?"

Uncle Alec nodded. "Yes, he is. He recently moved to the Hamptons in an effort to see more of his kids. Though I'm not sure if his ex-wife was all that happy about it."

"Why don't we interview the placard swinger first and then look into the ex-husband?"

"I already set up an appointment," said her uncle. "You'll see him this afternoon. And now you better interview Alpin before he talks God into rescuing him from his cell." He gave Odelia a wink. "Or talks to his lawyer, which is more likely."

They both sat down in front of the irate publisher, who sat shackled to the table in the interview room. His hair was mussed and he was sporting a bloody nose and a black eye but otherwise appeared to have calmed down considerably since his run-in with Chase's fist.

"Look, I can't be in here," he said the moment Odelia and Chase walked in. "I have meetings to attend—plus, I have to take my daughter to her ballet lesson and my son to his little league game—I'm also the trainer, you see, so I can't afford to be late. A dozen kids are counting on me."

"You should have thought of that before you assaulted a police officer," said Chase gravely.

"I—I wasn't thinking, okay?" asked the guy, running a hand through his red mane. "I just wanted to talk to Donna. She's been fighting us on this wall issue for months and frankly I'm fed up."

"What's the story behind this wall?" asked Odelia.

Alpin sighed. "About a year ago Donna filed the necessary paperwork to build an extension on the west side of her current property, adjacent to mine. At first all she wanted was to build a gazebo, which was fine by me, even though it would have been right next to my pool. So I called her and asked her if she was going to throw parties at this gazebo or what? She said she was building it as a temple of solitude—a place for her to meditate in peace and quiet. So I gave her my blessing and said to knock herself out. Only she must have realized she wasn't going to get a lot of peace and quiet if she was building this temple of solitude twenty yards from my pool, so she filed new plans, which included a twenty-foot wall!"

"That's… high," said Odelia.

The man scoffed, "You don't say! That monstrosity was going to block out my sun. Right next to my pool! And then she came up with a plan to extend this wall all around her property, which would affect not just me but two of her other neighbors as well. And to make matters worse she was also going to cut an access road that is used by pretty much the entire neighborhood. So as you can imagine, the neighborhood association wasn't too happy about this."

"Did you try and talk her out of it?"

"Yes, I did. We all did. We organized a meet, but she never showed up. Instead, she sent her lawyer, who said we didn't have a leg to stand on and that her client was adamant to go through with her plans regardless our protestations."

"What did the council say?"

"Apparently they were all big fans of Donna's cause they told us she had every right to put in place measures that would increase her sense of safety and security. There had been several threats made against the lady's life and she was forced to tighten security measures." He held up his hand. "Which I totally understand. But not at the expense of the entire neighborhood. I'm sure that if we could have sat down with Donna and talked things through, we could have made her see reason. Instead she chose to bulldoze her plans through and shove them down our throats!"

"And you weren't having it."

"Damn straight we weren't having it!"

"So you killed her," said Chase.

The man's face morphed into an expression of shock. "Killed her?!"

"At seven o'clock this morning you attacked Donna Bruce and murdered her."

"Murdered her! Donna was… murdered?!"

"Oh, come off it, Mr. Carré. You know very well what happened. You were there."

"No, I wasn't! I—I didn't even know she was dead."

"Why did you think the police were at the scene?"

The man's jaw had dropped and he hitched it up with some effort. "I just figured you were there to protect her from… us."

"Where were you this morning at seven, Mr. Carré?"

"I was home, preparing for the demonstration. Just ask my neighbors. We were putting together…" He cut a quick look to Chase. "… placards."

Chase rubbed his head where the placard had struck and gave the other man a dirty look. "Are you sure you didn't sneak out at some point to lock Mrs. Bruce up inside her sauna cabin and unleash a bunch of bees on her?"

"Bees? Of course not. Where would I get a bunch of bees?"

"At the bee farm."

"Look," he said, licking his lips nervously. "Talk to my neighbors. Or my wife, for that matter. I was right there—up at the crack of dawn, on the phone with the other guys, and we all met at six to start preparations for the demonstration.

We weren't going to let Donna pull a fast one on us. We were going to take this thing to court if we had to. I still hoped she would listen to reason once she realized she was antagonizing the entire neighborhood. But I swear to God, I would never kill her!"

"Do you have any idea who would have?" asked Odelia.

He thought for a moment. "Well, like I said, death threats had been made against her."

"Any idea who made them?"

"There was this producer whose career she ruined. Um, what's his name…" He snapped his fingers, then his face cleared. "Ransom Montlló. I remember because his name came up when we were in talks to turn *The Shed* into a motion picture. The guy's a washout, though. Nobody will work with him. And he's got Donna Bruce to thank for that."

"So it's true that *The Shed* is going to be a movie?"

The man smiled for the first time. "I'm afraid I can't discuss the particulars but so far it's looking pretty good."

"And George Clooney is attached to play God?"

His smile widened. "I cannot confirm or deny anything."

Chase made a sound of disgust and got up. "Please don't leave town, Mr. Carré. We're not through with you yet."

"Look, I'm sorry, all right?" the publisher said, holding up a hand in a gesture of appeasement. "I'm not normally a violent man, but Donna had us with our backs against the wall—no pun intended. We were just trying to protect the neighborhood. I'm sorry about your head, dude."

"That's all right," Odelia said. "Chase has a thick skull. I'm sure you didn't even make a dent."

Chase made a growling sound at the back of his throat, and Odelia decided that perhaps it would be best not to poke the bear. So she also got up and thanked Alpin Carré for his time. The man frowned. "So… am I under arrest here or what?"

"Yes," said Chase.

"No," said Odelia.

The publisher looked from one to the other. "Um, so what is it?"

Chase threw up his hands and walked out. Odelia gave Alpin her best smile. "You're free to go, Mr. Carré. But if I could make a suggestion, maybe next time try not to hit a cop. They don't like it."

He returned her smile. "You are by far the nicest cop I've ever met."

"Oh, but I'm not a cop. I'm just a consultant."

"That explains everything," he said, and shook her hand warmly. "Seriously, though. Look into Ransom Montlló. The guy had a serious grudge against Donna."

"Even more than you?"

"I might hold a grudge but I would never kill a person."

"And Ransom Montlló would?"

"Well, the guy was a green beret. He's got the skills."

"How come you know so much about him?"

"He used to live two doors down from me. But that was before Donna came into his life."

CHAPTER 8

We were finally on our way to Vena Aleman. Me and Dooley had fought Odelia tooth and claw, but there was no use. We were going to the vet no matter what. At least Brutus and Harriet had been saved—for now. They were going next week, as Vena was too busy to see four cats at once. But for Dooley and I there was no reprieve.

On the drive over, we discussed the case. When Odelia mentioned the producer and the publisher and the ex-husband who had it in for Donna, I thought it was starting to look like Donna Bruce was one of those people who had rubbed everyone the wrong way and had made a lot of enemies on her way to the top.

"So either one of them could have done it?" I asked.

"Well, except for the publisher. Chase talked to some of the neighbors and they all swear up and down that Alpin couldn't have done it."

"What about the bees?" I asked. "How did they get the bees?"

"Good question," said Odelia, unhurriedly steering the pickup out of town. "The beekeeper the bees were stolen from had equipped his hives with a GPS tracker. So when he got the message one of his hives was on the move, he immediately contacted the police. This happened around six this morning. He found his pallet discarded behind Donna's house, the bees in the sauna cabin—at least the ones that survived."

"Did he get his bees back?" asked Dooley, sounding worried.

"Yes, he did. Though a lot of them died. When a bee stings they usually don't survive the sting. And the heat of the sauna didn't do much for their wellbeing either."

"But who would do such a thing?" asked Dooley, aghast. "To harm those innocent creatures like that?"

Odelia shook her head. "No idea, Dooley. But whoever it was, they must have had some knowledge about handling bees. At least that's what the beekeeper told Chase."

I thought about this for a moment. "Do you think there's a significance to this? I mean, why not simply shoot the woman, or hit her over the head with a mallet? Why go to all the trouble of stealing a bunch of bees—"

"More like thousands of bees," Odelia interjected.

"—and running the risk of being found before you can carry out your plan?"

She smiled. "And that's why I want the four of you to work together. You all bring something unique and special to this investigation."

"So you agree Harriet wouldn't be able to handle this on her own?"

"None of us can handle this on our own, Max. Though I would like you to give Harriet a chance. Let her run with this for a while. See where it takes you guys."

I frowned. This wasn't what I'd wanted to hear. "But I'm in charge, right? I'm the one who takes the lead."

"Not this time. Harriet is going to be running point,"

Odelia said. "And you follow her lead. I want to see where she will take the investigation."

"But I thought you said she couldn't do this on her own."

"She can't. She needs you, Max—and Dooley, of course. I want you to work as a team. Can you do that for me?"

"I suppose," I said reluctantly. "But I still don't see—"

"Harriet needs you, Max. She needs your intelligence and your skill. The thing is, I want to see her blossom. Reach her full potential. Harriet has a lot to offer. But, like I said, she can't do this all by herself. And that's where you come in. You and Dooley."

"Me, too?" asked Dooley, delighted.

"Of course! You guys are my A team. My main sleuths."

I thought about this for a moment, and then I saw what Odelia was trying to say. Officially, she was putting Harriet in charge, but in actual fact I would be the one in charge, as usual. She just wanted Harriet to *think* she was in charge, to boost her self-confidence and to give her something to do other than run around with Brutus and make a total fool of herself. So I winked at Odelia. "I get it," I finally said. "Harriet is in charge, but really *I'm* in charge, huh?"

"No, Harriet is in charge, Max."

I laughed. "Sure. She's 'in charge' but I'm *in charge*. Gotcha."

"Whatever you say, Max," she said, and parked the car. "And here we are."

My smile vanished. "Eep."

Odelia had brought along our cat boxes, though I'd assured her this wasn't necessary. We would walk into Vena's on our own four paws, head held high, pride intact. But Odelia didn't seem to trust my word or Dooley's, for she shoved us into our respective carriers and then we were off. God. This was so humiliating...

Once inside, she parked us on the floor and went off in search of Vena.

"I don't like this, Max," said Dooley as he looked out at me through the slats. "I don't like this at all."

"Me neither," I intimated. "It's like we're prisoners all of a sudden."

"We are prisoners. About to be prodded and poked and stabbed with needles."

I closed my eyes. I hated needles so much just the thought made me weak at the knees. Not that I had any chance of standing up in this cramped box. Dooley, who's a lot smaller than me, at least had some wiggle room, while I filled out this entire box. My butt was pushed up against the back, my nose against the front, and I could hardly move. Good thing I'm not claustrophobic! And to think Odelia said she got me the biggest carrier she could find. I'd already told her she should have gotten me a dog carrier. They come in the bigger sizes. But she said she still had to be able to carry me.

Just then, another person came in, carrying a box containing a scared-looking cat. I knew that cat. It was Shanille, the conductor of cat choir, and the person carrying her was none other than Father Reilly himself.

"Hey, Shanille," I said. "So you're up for it, too, huh?"

"Hey, Max," she said softly. "Dooley. Yeah, I fought hard, but to no avail."

"You're not sick or anything are you?"

"Sick? Why would I be sick? I'm the healthiest cat alive. No, I've got a tick."

I frowned. "A tick? What's a tick?"

"Beats me. Father Reilly says I have a tick, so we had to come to Vena to get rid of it."

"It's a heart condition," said Dooley. "Has to be. Humans call the heart the ticker. What Father Reilly probably meant to say was that you have a problem with your ticker."

"I don't have a problem with my ticker! My ticker is just fine. He said tick, not ticker."

"Yeah, Dooley," I said. "If it was her ticker they wouldn't want to get rid of it, would they?"

"Unless her ticker is broken. They'd want to replace it with another ticker." His eyes suddenly went wide. "Oh, God. Is that why I'm here? They're going to remove my ticker and put it in Shanille? But I don't want to die! I'm too young to die!"

"Tick, not ticker," I reminded him. "A tick is obviously not a ticker, so your ticker is perfectly safe."

He didn't seem to buy it, still looking worried. "We should Google it," he said. "The Google knows everything. The Google knows what a tick is."

"It's not *the* Google, Dooley," I said. "It's Google, without the article."

"What article?"

"Forget about it."

"So what are you guys here for?" asked Shanille.

"Me, to have my tick removed and implanted in you," said Dooley dully, "and Max to have his morbid obesity taken care of."

"I'm not morbidly obese! I'm big. It's genetic."

"You have gained a lot of weight, Max," said Shanille. "You should probably go on a diet."

"I'm not going on a diet! I hate diets! And I'm not over-weight. I'm just big, that's all."

"You don't even fit in that cage. You're pressed up against the sides like a balloon. You look like something that exploded inside that cage and is now sticking to the sides."

"Nice, Shanille. And here I thought you were my friend," I grumbled.

"I'm just looking out for you. At the rate you're going you're going to have trouble with your ticker soon. I know because Vena told me last time I had an enlarged heart and I had to go on a diet."

"You don't look overweight," said Dooley. "In fact you look just fine."

"I know, right? That's because I went on the diet."

"Look, my ticker is fine," I insisted, not liking the direction this conversation had taken.

"Oh, my God!" Dooley screamed. "They're going to take my ticker and implant it in you, aren't they?! Because your ticker is on the fritz. That's why I'm here! I'm gonna die!"

"Nobody is going to have their ticker removed, Dooley," I said with an eyeroll. "My ticker is fine, your ticker is fine, and Shanille's ticker is fine. See? We're all fine."

"Except that I have trouble with my tick," said Shanille.

"I'm pretty sure that's not a life-threatening thing," I said.

"You never know," said Dooley, still panting hard. He was looking around nervously, at the posters on the wall warning pet owners about the various diseases they needed to monitor their dearly beloved pets for. "I could have rabies, or an upper respiratory tract infection, or kidney failure, or ringworm or zoonosis or hookworm infection or toxocariasis or gingivitis or giardiasis or sporotrichosis or bartonellosis—"

"Stop, stop!" Shanille yelled. "You're making me sick."

"I know! That's because we *are* sick! Why else would we be at the vet?!"

"We're just here for our annual checkup," I reminded him. "Just like humans have to visit the dentist once a year, we visit Vena once a year. That doesn't mean we're sick or dying. That just means Odelia wants to make sure we're fine, all right? She loves us and wants to take care of us."

"All right," he said, settling down somewhat. Then his eye fell on one particular poster and he gave a loud yelp. "Tick—tick—tick!" he cried, pointing his paw.

Shanille and I looked in the direction indicated and saw a large picture of the most horrible creature I'd ever seen in my entire life. It looked like a giant red spider, and it was burrowing into the skin of some poor hapless pet. "Oh my God!" I squeaked.

But Shanille shrieked the loudest. "Get it off me! Get it off! Get it off! Get it off!"

"Get away from me!" Dooley squealed, trying to shift his cage further away from Shanille's by rocking back and forth. "Help! Help! It's gonna jump on me—I can feel it! Help me!" Finally, he managed to overturn his cage, toppling to the floor. Unfortunately, it toppled the wrong way, and now he was right next to Shanille and screaming even louder. "It's crawling all over me!" he screamed. "I can feel its claws digging in! Heeeeelp!"

Suddenly Odelia, Father Reilly and Vena appeared in the doorway, alerted by the loud cries of three felines. Only Odelia could understand us, of course, and when she did, she had to suppress a chuckle. To her credit, she took immediate action. She righted Dooley's carrier, then lifted mine, and carried us both into Vena's consultation room. Off we were, into the lion's den…

CHAPTER 9

"*T*hey're dying to see you," Odelia told Vena. "In fact they were so anxious they were meowing up a storm."

"Liar," I said, but she ignored me.

Dooley was still frantically scratching himself all over. "The tick!" he cried. "The tick is on me! It's got me!"

"There is no tick on you," I said. "If that tick has dug itself into Shanille it's not going to jump ship. Shanille is way tastier than you."

"She is not!" Dooley said indignantly, but he seemed quietly relieved. I think he probably knew that if a tick has a choice between Shanille and him, there's no question.

"So. My two favorite cats!" Vena said, planting her hands on her sizable hips. Vena is a big and powerfully built woman, cast from the same mold that has produced the likes of Arnold Schwarzenegger and John Cena. Then again, if you're going to pull calves from cows you probably have to have superhuman strength.

"Hi, Vena," I said quietly.

She grunted approvingly. "I think he likes me, Odelia."

"Oh, he loves you. They both do. In fact they can't wait to come and see you."

"And with good reason! They know I've got their best interests in mind!" She laughed loudly, and snapped the latches on our carriers, then picked me up and placed me on the examination table.

I gulped as I plunked down. I knew I had no other choice. If I tried to escape she would simply grab me by the scruff of the neck and haul me back. And that's when the prodding and the poking began, just like I'd anticipated.

"Shouldn't she be doing me first?" asked Dooley. "The tick…"

"There is no tick!" I yelled, losing my patience. In my defense, I was under extreme duress, as Vena's hands had just prodded me in the belly, one of my many sensitive areas.

She proceeded to pull my ears, check inside them with a flashlight—probably in search of hidden treasure—and wrench my mouth open to check my teeth. All the while, she made these low grunting sounds that scared the bejeezus out of me. Finally, she placed some kind of round metal object against my chest, stuck what looked like a pair of earphones into her ears and frowned thoughtfully.

"Ha ha!" I yelped as she dug that metal thing into my fur. "It tickles!"

She staunchly ignored me, Odelia's hands firmly holding me down, Vena listening intently. I remembered from last time she was only trying to listen to my heartbeat but it was still scary.

"Myes. Myes," the vet finally muttered. "Just what I thought. Your cat is fat, Odelia."

"What?!" I cried. "Not true! I'm big-boned! It runs in the family!"

"I know," said Odelia, gently stroking my fur. "I noticed this morning when he had trouble jumping up on the bed."

"The mattress became bigger overnight!"

"Yep," said Vena, patting my head. "That is one obese tabby."

"It's the breed! I'm a tiger cat. We're big. We have to be, so we can prowl the jungle."

"Is that true?" asked Dooley from the floor. "Are you really a tiger cat?"

"It's something I read on The Google," I said desperately.

"I thought it was just Google, without the article?"

"Shut up, Dooley! I'm fighting for my life here!"

"I indulge him too much, don't I?" asked Odelia.

"Don't beat yourself up, honey," said Vena. "A lot of people do. But he has to go back on a diet, I'm afraid. If not, all that fat is going to start taxing his heart. I can hear a definite murmur, which tells me his heart has to work too hard. Over time, he might also develop diabetes and a host of other ailments. So if you want to keep your Max happy and healthy, you're going to have to do the work."

"I am happy," I said, though that stuff about diabetes and murmurs kinda gave me pause.

"Did you hear that, Max?" asked Odelia, bending down to look into my eyes. "If I want you happy and healthy I'm going to have to put you on a diet. And you know what that means."

"Oh, God, not again," I muttered.

"I love you, Max. I don't want you to get sick on me, you hear? I need you fit and healthy."

"I hear you," I said resignedly. Murmurs and diabetes? Who needs that crap?

"Do you still remember what you gave him last year?" Vena asked.

"I think I kept the receipt." And while she and Vena

worked out my diet, I jumped from the examination table. I landed with a dull thud, and Odelia looked down, then nodded. "Yep. Too fat."

"I'm sorry, Max," said Dooley commiseratingly. "If you want, you can have some of my food."

"No, I better not," I said, plunking down on the floor. To be honest, I was starting to feel the strain of carrying all this extra weight around. Vena was probably right. I wasn't as agile as I used to be, and it wasn't a lot of fun. And I had an obligation as a feline sleuth to help Odelia, and I couldn't do that if I couldn't even chase suspects around now could I?

"So you're actually going to do this?" asked Dooley.

"Yep. Looks like I am." I heaved a deep sigh. "The things I do for my human…"

And then it was Dooley's turn. He was picked up and subjected to a similar examination. When it was all over, he asked in a tremulous voice, "Am I going to die?"

Odelia smiled. "What's the verdict, Vena?"

"He's a little too scrawny for my taste," said the doctor. "Not enough muscle tissue. I think he needs to go on a diet, too. Only a protein-building diet."

"Oh, God—I don't want to go on a diet!" Dooley cried. "I'm not fat!"

"You're going to have to eat more, Dooley," Odelia said.

He abruptly stopped his whimpering. "Eat more?"

"You're too skinny."

"Too skinny? Is that even possible?"

"What about parasites?" asked Odelia. "Or ticks?"

"He's perfectly fine—they both are," the doctor assured Odelia. "But like I said, Max is too fat and Dooley is too skinny. So you're going to have to put them both on a diet."

And thus ended our annual visit to the vet. Dooley was going to have to eat more and me… less. Bummer! Then again, it could have been worse. We could have suffered from any of the diseases listed in Vena's waiting room. Or… ticks. And as we rode back home with Odelia, I shivered when I thought of Shanille. There would be no more choir practice for a while. At least until I was reasonably sure that Vena had taken care of our conductor's tick problem. Brrrr!

CHAPTER 10

*O*delia thought it was a little awkward to go the gym in the middle of a murder investigation, especially since she'd already spent so much time with the cats at Vena's, but a promise was a promise. She and Chase had decided to be gym buddies and there was no way she was going to weasel out now.

She'd dumped her gym gear into the pickup before she set out for the vet, and now parked her car in front of the gym, which was located in a strip mall just outside of town. The same strip mall housed what had once been The Vitamin King, a health food store operated by Donovan Rubb, who'd used it to sell drugs and other illegal substances beneath the counter. Since Rubb was busted, the store now housed a nail salon, and not a bad one either.

She let the cats out of the car. They could use some fresh air after the ordeal they'd gone through at the hands of Vena. They'd taken it well, she thought, all things considered, and she had to resist the urge to buy them both a treat. No more junk food. From now on, they were going on a strict diet, Dooley to bulk up and Max to slim down.

She slung her gym bag over her shoulder and walked up to Triple Platinum Gym. It was rumored that some of the celebrities that visited the Hamptons trained here, or at least the ones who didn't have a private gym installed at their multi-million-dollar mansions. She looked up when the roar of a motorcycle sounded behind her, and a leather-clad biker rode up on a powerful machine. He waved at her so she waved back, wondering if this could be Brad Pitt or Leonardo DiCaprio, ready to lift some weights. When the biker removed his helmet and shook out his shoulder-length hair, however, a smile curled up her lips.

"Hey, Chase. You certainly know how to make an entrance."

He directed a cheeky grin at her, his eyes smiling. "Thanks. So are you ready for the workout from hell?"

"I'm ready for a workout, without the hell. I haven't been to the gym in years," she reminded him, "so go easy on me, will you?"

"Sure thing, babe," he growled and stepped from his machine.

She frowned. When had he started calling her babe? Maybe since they'd started kissing as if it was a regular thing?

He walked up to her and bent over, planting a wet smooch on her lips that made her stomach perform a double flip. Then he pulled her against his black leather jacket and repeated the procedure, only this time putting some tongue into play. When he finally released her, she thought she heard tweety-birds singing in a nearby tree. It could have been her imagination.

"Let's go, babe," he said, slinging an arm around her and directing her inside.

The gym was crowded, its patrons the usual mix of hot-looking trim chicks and equally hot-looking buff dudes.

People were grunting as they hoisted stacks of iron while others were shedding what could have been their body weight in sweat as they raced an imaginary opponent on the stationary bike while watching *Keeping Up with the Kardashians* on the overhead TV screens. Loud rock music was blaring, the sound mixing with that of the TV screens, and somewhere near the back the Hells Angels seemed to be holding a convention, as pony-tailed middle-aged men were encouraging other pony-tailed middle-aged men to put in 'one more rep, Rudy!' Odelia smiled. She hadn't realized how much she'd missed the club.

She said goodbye to Chase as she headed into the locker room and when she re-emerged, dressed in obligatory skintight lycra in the prerequisite loud colors, she saw that Chase had already reserved a station for them. It was the cable pulley machine for the back, and Chase was pulling down on the wide iron bar, the muscles in his back well-defined. She expelled an involuntary gasp. The man was huge! Dressed in a tank top and biker shorts, he was also exceedingly hot, and she had to resist the urge to stare at his pronounced front bump.

"You started without me," she said as she walked up.

He grinned and let the weights fall down on the stack with a loud clanging sound. "Just a few warmup reps. So what do you wanna do?"

"I thought about limiting myself to the cross trainer today. Start building up that cardiovascular endurance again."

"Or we could do some weight training first, and then finish off the session with some cardio."

She shrugged. She wasn't exactly a pro at this kind of stuff, and he definitely had more experience. "Have you been doing this long?"

"I started when I was sixteen, so you might say that's a

long time. My dad used to take me to the gym. I was a skinny kid and he thought I could use some bulking up. And since I was also a shy kid I was being bullied a lot and he figured some weight training might help with that as well."

"And did it help?"

"It did. Most bullies are cowards. They don't like to pick on guys that are bigger than them. And it didn't take me long to get a lot bigger. Of course I had a strong incentive. These days I just do it to stay healthy and strong."

"So no ambitions to compete?" she asked, pointing at a poster announcing an upcoming bodybuilding competition.

"Hell, no," he said with a laugh. "To be absolutely honest I'm not sure it's entirely healthy to do this stuff professionally. It's a completely different ballgame."

"It sure is," she said as she watched a guy as big as a house pose in front of the mirror. With his veins popping and his muscles clearly visible beneath his skin, he looked a little scary. "So what did you have in mind, coach?"

"Sit yourself down, little lady," he said with a drawl, "and I'll tell you exactly what I have in mind."

So she sat down, and after he'd changed the pin in the stack, she grabbed the handles and pulled down hard. It took her some time to get into the groove again, but then she remembered this had always been one of her favorite machines, and soon she could feel her blood pumping and her heart pounding. It was a great feeling and she gave Chase a grateful smile. "This feels good!"

"Of course it does."

She wiped her sweat with her towel and they headed for the next machine, this time focusing on chest muscles. And as they walked from machine to machine, doing a full back and chest workout, she said, "There's been a lot of rumors going around."

"Oh? About what?"

"About us."

Chase was lying on a low bench, pressing two dumbbells up in a lateral motion. "Us, huh?"

"Yep," she said as casually as possible.

"And what are they saying?"

"Well, 'they' seem to think we're in a hurry to tie the knot."

"And is there a reason for all this hurry?" he asked with a grunt as he lowered the dumbbells.

"They think I'm pregnant and wouldn't like to walk down the aisle with a baby bump."

He grinned as he sat upright, toweling his face. "Pregnant, huh? What do you know?"

"Yeah. It came as something of a surprise, to be honest."

"Not to me."

"It doesn't?"

"Nope. I think when you take into consideration how those two lovebirds have been behaving—kissing any chance they get—it's hardly surprising an accident would happen. And a shotgun wedding is the only way to go to spare the parents the embarrassment."

"Those two lovebirds, huh?"

"Yep."

"Kissing all over town."

"That's right."

"Strange. As far as I know they haven't even gone on their first date yet, not to mention that she is not aware of the way he feels about her as he hasn't said a peep."

"Not a peep, huh?"

"Not a single squeak."

"What if I were to tell you that he figures all those times he joined her for dinner at her parents' place counted as so many dates? And that the reason he hasn't told her how he feels is that he didn't want to rush into things?"

"I'm sure she doesn't count a dinner at her folks as a date, seeing how she didn't even invite him but he more or less was her uncle's plus-one. And as for rushing into things, he should keep in mind that she's perfectly capable of telling him when she's feeling rushed and so far she's feeling anything but rushed. Quite the opposite. She's starting to wonder if he has any feelings for her at all."

They stared at each other for a moment, then Chase took out his water bottle and quaffed deeply. "You know what?" he asked when he was done. "I think you're right. Tagging along as your uncle's plus-one doesn't constitute a date. So why don't I ask you out on a proper date right here, right now? Odelia Poole? Will you join me for dinner and a movie?"

She smiled. "I'll think about it."

"Why, you…" He made a grab for her but she deftly avoided his hands and fluttered off with a giggle. When she looked back, he was chasing her, a playful expression on his face. She squealed and darted away towards the back of the gym, stared after by the troop of Hells Angels, who seemed to enjoy the spectacle, judging from their loud cheers.

She flew out the back door and found herself in a small courtyard, where some old iron barbells and benches stood, probably used by the most hardcore fitness fanatics. As it was, the courtyard was empty, and as she searched around for an escape route, Chase was already upon her. He swept her up in his arms, and then kissed her deeply. She went under and gave herself up to his passionate embrace. There was nothing equivocal about his kisses this time. The man might not be great with words but his lips still told her everything she needed to know. As did his hands, which quickly roamed to places they'd never roamed before. And she wouldn't have minded if he lay her down on one of the benches right now and had his way with her, if not a choir of voices suddenly alerted her to the fact that they were no longer alone.

"Why are Chase and Odelia fighting?" asked Dooley.

"They're not fighting, Dooley," said Max. "They're kissing."

"Kissing? But then why are his hands all over her?"

"That's all part of the ritual. Humans who like each other touch each other all over."

"Gran likes Odelia but I've never seen her touch her like this."

"I think it's romantic," Harriet gushed. "The most romantic thing I've ever seen."

"I think it's disgusting," said Brutus in his gruff voice.

"Brutus! It's love!"

"It's a lot of bodily fluids going into a lot of weird places. It's unhygienic is what it is."

"Brutus! You're a brute!"

With extreme regret, Odelia extricated herself from Chase. It was a little hard to be caught up in the moment with this Greek choir commenting on her every move.

"Something wrong?" asked Chase, his face flushed.

She gestured with her head to the four cats, who sat on top of the wall looking down at them.

"That's just a bunch of cats, babe."

"That's a bunch of my cats."

He looked again and did a double take. "Christ, you're right. What are they doing here?"

"I took Max and Dooley to the vet. Brutus and Harriet must have wandered off on their own." She could hardly explain to Chase how the foursome was eager to solve the murder of Donna Bruce. She sat upright, pushing at her blond bob and adjusting her top, which had slid down with a little help from Chase.

Chase looked like he wanted to chase the cats away, but

managed to resist the urge. He cleared his throat. "So what about that date, huh?"

"I would love to," she said gratefully.

He smiled broadly. "Then it's a date. Oh, and Odelia?"

"Mh?"

He fixed her with an intent look. "I like you. I like you a lot."

She returned his smile and took his face in her hands. "I like you, Chase. Very much."

And then they kissed again, only a little less exuberantly than before, but no less heartfelt.

"Aah," Harriet gushed.

"Ugh," Brutus groaned.

CHAPTER 11

*W*e all rode home with Odelia. She was very chirpy after her time spent at the gym. I thought it probably had something to do with hormones. When humans work out, they release something called endorphins in their brains, which make them feel happy. Or it might be all the kissing and groping she was doing with Chase. If this kept up, she'd soon have babies, which is something that tends to happen when humans kiss a lot. Female humans suddenly have baby humans. I have to admit I was not looking forward to that at all. I kinda liked the arrangement we had right now: me, Odelia and Dooley had a great thing going here. We didn't need another little human to come in and ruining everything. Not to mention that Chase would move in and seriously cramp up our style.

Odelia was so happy she had a stupid grin on her face all the way home, and didn't say a word.

"So what did you find out about the murderer?" I finally asked, deciding that someone had to take things in hand and steer them on the right track again.

"Huh?" asked Odelia, snapping out of whatever daydream she was living.

"The Donna thing? We are still trying to find out who killed that poor woman, aren't we?"

Odelia looked at Harriet, whose turn it was to ride shotgun, the three of us ensconced on the backseat. "What have you found out so far, Harriet?"

Harriet seemed taken aback. She probably hadn't expected that leading an investigation was going to involve actual, you know, leading an investigation. "I, um…" she began, darting a desperate look at Brutus. But that big lug wasn't much help either, as he just sat there, lost in thought. Probably still trying to get the image of Odelia and Chase out of his mind. I didn't blame him. Watching humans smooch is a traumatic experience.

"Um…" Harriet repeated. Then she seemed to get an idea, judging from the way her furry face suddenly lit up with what might be termed the light of intelligence. Though it might also have been gas. "We could do an Internet search!" she exclaimed.

Odelia's eyebrows rose. "An Internet search?"

"Yeah. Donna Bruce was an Internet entrepreneur, so there's bound to be a lot of stuff about her on the Internet."

"Oh, I'm sure there is," said Odelia, though she sounded a little disappointed. When you have four feline sleuths at your disposal, an Internet search isn't exactly what you're looking for. She probably could do all the Internet searches she wanted to do herself. But being the good sport that she was, she smiled at Harriet and said, "Knock yourself out, honey."

Harriet beamed, directing a triumphant look at me. I held up my paw, claw up, in a sign of appreciation, but under my breath I told Dooley, "What a chump."

"Huh?" asked Dooley, waking up from a stupor.

"Harriet is going to do an Internet search on Donna. She

hopes to find the killer that way," I told him, just in case he hadn't been following the conversation, which obviously he hadn't. "And Odelia thinks it's just the way to go."

"And isn't it?"

"Of course not. What are we going to find on the Internet that will lead us to the killer? I mean, it's not as if whoever murdered Donna posted a message online announcing the fact. Nobody is that dumb."

"Right," said Dooley, descending into his stupor again.

I frowned at him. "What's the matter with you? You're awfully quiet all of a sudden."

Dooley nodded. "Right," he muttered, clearly not listening to a word I said.

I gave him a nudge. "Hey. What's going on with you?"

He looked up. "Mh? Oh. I was just thinking is all."

That immediately had me worried. When Dooley starts thinking, it's bad news, as his cerebral capacity is too limited to allow for more than the occasional fleeting thought about food. It was obvious he was overtaxing his brain in a way that could prove detrimental. "Thinking about what?"

"Do you think Odelia and Chase are going to be married?" he asked finally.

"Yes, I do," I said, understanding dawning. He'd been thinking along the same lines I had.

"I mean, what with all that kissing that was going on back there... The next step is usually that they get married, right?"

"I'm afraid so," I said with a sigh.

"So who's going to give Odelia away?" he asked. "I know she'll probably ask you, seeing as that you're her cat and all, but I consider myself her cat, too, and I love her a lot, so I would like to be considered for the honor as well."

I looked up sharply. "That's what you're worried about?!"

He nodded sheepishly. "You're my best friend, Max, but giving Odelia away would be like a dream come true. And since I figure she's not the type to get married more than once, this is a once-in-a-lifetime opportunity, so…"

I rolled my eyes. I saw what was going on. Marge was a big fan of the Hallmark Channel, and Dooley must have caught a lot of those slushy romantic movies lately, and gotten the idea in his head he was supposed to give away the bride or something. "Look, Dooley," I said, wondering how to launch into this without upsetting him. "The thing is that in this tradition it's not the woman's cat who gives her away. At least not to my knowledge."

He frowned. "But I thought it was the one who loved her the most who gave her away? And there's no one who loves Odelia more than me."

"Well, I love Odelia a lot."

"Oh, I know that. But I love her more."

"How do you reckon that?"

"I just have a more loving personality, I guess. You have to admit that you can be something of a curmudgeon some-times, Max. I mean, you live with Odelia and probably don't appreciate what you've got. Since I don't live with Odelia, but still get to spend a lot of time with her, I obviously appreciate her a lot more, which means I also love her a lot more."

"That's just not true!" I said a little heatedly. "I appreciate Odelia just as much as you do, maybe even more, and I love her more because she's my human, not yours."

Dooley raised his chin. "She may not *technically* be my human, but since I'm more lovable she loves me a lot more than she loves you."

"*You're* more lovable? *I'm* more lovable! And Odelia loves *me* the most."

"She does not. She loves me the most!"

"Does not!"

"Does too!"

"Not!"

"Too!"

"Guys, guys!" said Odelia, who must have overheard the discussion. She glanced at us through the rearview mirror. "Let's keep it civil."

"Odelia, Dooley says he loves you more than me," I complained. "But that's not possible, is it?"

"You're arguing over who loves me more? Aww, that's so sweet," said Odelia.

"I love you the most," said Dooley, "which means I get to give you away, right?"

"Give me away? Why would you want to get rid of me? I thought you just said you loved me."

"It's a tradition. Marge told me all about it. When a woman gets married, the one who loves her the most gives her away to the guy she's getting married to. And since you're getting married to Chase, I want to be the one to give you away."

Odelia laughed. "Dooley, I'm touched that you would want to do that, but first of all, I'm not getting married anytime soon."

"You're not?"

"No, I'm not. And secondly, I'm pretty sure my dad would like to give me away. That's also part of the tradition."

"Your dad?" asked Dooley, disappointed.

"See?" I said. "I told you."

"You're not getting married?" asked Harriet, also entering the discussion.

"No, of course not. Who said anything about getting married?"

"But... you were kissing Chase."

Odelia smiled indulgently. "Look, I like Chase. I like him a lot. And because I like him so much, I also enjoy kissing him. That's what humans do. But that doesn't mean I'm going to marry him."

"Oh," said Harriet, looking confused. She'd obviously been watching the same goop as Dooley. Damn that Hallmark Channel. Putting all these weird ideas in cats' heads.

"I still think it's disgusting," Brutus muttered, making a face. "Yuck."

"Brutus!" Harriet cried. "It's not disgusting. It's beautiful." She sighed. "It's love."

"Well, not love, exactly," I said. "It's more a matter of hormones."

"Oh, it is, is it?" asked Odelia with a laugh.

"Yeah. I don't know how it works, exactly, but I'm pretty sure pheromones feature into the thing pretty heavily." See? I don't watch the Hallmark Channel but the Discovery Channel. That's why I'm smart and the others are all dummies.

"It's not all about pheromones, Max," said Odelia softly, and she got that faraway look in her eyes again. I didn't know why she got that look, but I'm pretty sure it had something with hormones, too. Whenever humans act funny, hormones are your safest bet. Just trust me on that.

We'd arrived home and Odelia dropped us off at the house. She walked in to get a bite to eat from the fridge and then installed us in front of the computer, so we could do 'Internet searches' to our hearts' content. And just when Harriet had clicked on her first key, the doorbell rang. And as Odelia went to answer it, the glass sliding door opened and Gran waltzed in. "Is he here?" she asked in that croaky voice of hers.

"Is who here?" I asked suspiciously. I just hoped Gran hadn't set up some kind of date with a man in Odelia's house. After all that kissing stuff back at the gym I didn't know how much more of this human lovemaking thing I could take right now.

"The UPS guy, of course. Who else?"

Just then, Odelia returned with a bulky package, a

puzzled look on her face. When she saw Gran, that puzzled look turned into one of concern. "Please tell me you didn't order any more Donna Bruce stuff, Gran."

"Of course I ordered more Donna Bruce stuff," Gran snapped. "I'm an old lady. I'm bored. I need to buy stuff so I can entertain myself. It's what old people do." She held up a bony finger. "And don't give me that you're-too-old-for-this-stuff crap. I get that enough from Tex. Now gimme." And with these words, she snatched the package from Odelia's hands and placed it on the living room table. In next to no time she ripped away the packaging and revealed the contents within.

I'd jumped down from the desk that held the computer and onto the chair that gave me a better vantage point to examine this new package. What I saw frankly worried me. There was a black mask, a whip of some kind, a pair of hand-cuffs, something that looked like a paddle, and a fuzzy, fluffy thing that may or may not have been a tickler. Huh?

Gran produced a fat chuckle and grabbed this new loot in her arms and started distributing it amongst the many pockets of her dress. "Pity Leo's gone. He would have loved this stuff."

"What is it?" asked Dooley.

She directed a keen look at him. "None of your business. You're a little too young to know."

"Are you going to arrest someone with those handcuffs?" asked Harriet.

"Sure. One hot stud—at least that's what I hope."

"Gran," said Odelia reproachfully. "You can't keep doing this. Dad's going to kill you when he finds out."

"Who's going to tell him?"

"He's going to know when he looks at his credit card bill."

"They don't itemize stuff. I'll just tell him it's adult diapers."

"He's your doctor. He would know if you needed adult diapers."

"I'll tell him it's preventive. What?" she added when Odelia gave her a critical look. "It never hurts to be careful about these things." She flicked the whip a few times, a look of relish on her wrinkled old face. "I'm gonna have so much fun!"

And then, before we could ask her any more questions, she was gone—out the door quick as a flash.

"I still don't get it," said Dooley. "That stuff is never featured on the Hallmark Channel."

"It's not on the Discovery Channel either," I said, equally puzzled. I turned to Odelia. "Is it featured on any channel?"

"Yeah, are we missing something?" asked Dooley.

Odelia smiled. "Oh, it's on a channel, all right, but not one destined for babies like you. Now, are you going to help me out with this Donna Bruce thing or not?"

Dutifully, we hopped down from the table and returned to our Internet search. Even with me and Dooley pooling our knowledge, gleaned from the Hallmark Channel and the Discovery Channel, there obviously was still a lot about the human experience that was alien to us. A lot of strange and wonderful things that were out there. But first… we had a murder to solve.

CHAPTER 12

*R*ansom Montlló lived in a dilapidated boarding house near the main road out of town. When Odelia and Chase arrived, a seedy-looking individual with a beer belly and a brown-bagged bottle of liquor in his hand sat playing fetch with his dog out on the front porch. He threw a stick in the direction of the road and the dog fetched it and returned it to the man's feet. Each time the dog ran off, the man took a swig from his bottle, then bent down to pick up the stick and threw it away again.

They mounted the creaky porch, avoiding the one broken step, and Chase brought out his police badge. "Are you the owner of this establishment, sir?"

"That, I'm not," said the man, slightly slurring his words.

"We're looking for Ransom Montlló."

"That, I am," said the man, and hiccuped. He frowned at Chase. "Am I in some kind of trouble, officer?" He held up his liquor bottle, wrapped in the brown paper bag. "This is not what it looks like."

"It's not?"

The man shook his head decidedly. "Apple juice. Just plain old apple juice."

"That's fine," said Chase, taking a seat next to the former producer. "I'm not interested in your juice, old-timer. My name is Chase Kingsley and this is Odelia Poole."

"Nice to meet you, missy," said Ransom, tipping an imaginary cap in Odelia's direction.

"We're looking into the murder of Donna Bruce."

The man's face turned into a scowl. "Donna Bruce? Someone murdered that old hag?"

"She wasn't that old," said Odelia.

"But she was a hag," said the man, nodding to add emphasis to his words.

"And why is that, exactly?" asked Chase.

"She went out and ruined me, didn't she?"

"What happened?" asked Odelia.

"Well, she was going to be in one of my movies. You may have heard of it. *A Star is Born.*"

Odelia frowned. "Wasn't that with Barbra Streisand and Kris Kristofferson?"

"There's also a version with Judy Garland and James Mason," said Chase.

She looked at him admiringly. "You know your classics."

"Big fan of old movies," he intimated.

"So we were shooting a new version," said Ransom, cutting through their chitchat, "and I had personally tapped Donna Bruce for the lead. I thought she'd be just great."

"I didn't know she could sing," said Odelia.

"Oh, she could sing all right."

"So she was really going to do this?" asked Odelia. "But I thought she retired from acting."

"This was way before that funny website she built," said the former producer. "Way, way before, back when the name Donna Bruce conjured up images of wonderful movies, and not golden dildos and the like." He chuckled freely, then dissolved into a coughing fit. When he came out of it, he continued, "So everything was set. We had our stars, we had our director, we had one of the major studios on board, and that's when tragedy struck."

"A storm?" asked Chase. "A freak storm destroyed the sets?"

"Not a storm."

"A stuntman died," said Odelia knowingly. "Or a stunt-woman. Donna's stunt double would have to be a woman, obviously."

"No one died," said the man, shuffling annoyedly.

"So what happened?" asked Chase.

"If you will just let me finish I'll tell you what the hell happened!"

"I'm sorry," said Chase. "Please continue."

"I will," he said, throwing the detective a look of censure. "Donna Bruce walked out, that's what happened. And since the studio was dead set on her, that was also the end of *A Star is Born*."

"Wait, she walked out of the movie?" asked Odelia.

"That's what I just said." He raked his fingers through his wild mane of gray hair. "Said she was sick and tired of being an actress and she was going to start a family instead. So she walked out of what would have been the best part of her career."

"So what did you do?"

"What could I do? I sued, of course!"

"You sued Donna Bruce?"

"Of course. She was ruining a movie I'd already sunk a big chunk of my own money in. So I sued." He sagged a little. "And lost."

Odelia glanced around at the rundown porch, paint peeling everywhere, the clapboards crooked and rotten in places, and the porch creaky and on the verge of collapse. "And then you ended up here," she said softly.

The man nodded and took a swig from his 'apple juice.' "Lost everything. My production company, my marriage, my life. And I've got Donna Bruce to thank for it."

"It's an odd coincidence that you ended up living not far from her, then," said Chase.

The man laughed a humorless, hacking laugh. "Me not living far from her? Her not living far from me! I was the first to discover Hampton Cove. Used to live down the lane from the Donna Bruce place, long before she ever moved here. This was when I was still a big shot in the movie business. I had a condo in New York, a mansion in LA, another mansion in Colorado, and a beach house in Florida." He gestured at the old porch. "Now this is my home, and Flea over there is my best friend."

Flea, who'd patiently been waiting for Ransom to throw the stick again, his tail pounding the floor and his tongue wagging excitedly, gave a short bark. Ransom picked up the stick and threw it as far as he could aim it, which was a little too close to the road this time. A truck came roaring up, just as Flea hurtled into the road to pick up his stick.

"Flea!" cried Ransom, rocketing up from his seat.

But luckily the dog was smarter than his owner, for he deftly avoided the truck's fender, waited patiently until he was safely out of the way, and then picked up his stick.

Ransom sat back down again, shaking his head. "Dumb dog," he muttered.

Dumb human, Odelia thought, also shaking her head.

"So where were you this morning between seven and eight, Mr. Montlló?" asked Chase.

"Right here on the porch, sipping my juice," said the producer. "Why do you want to know?"

"That's when Mrs. Bruce was murdered," said Chase.

"Murdered!" the producer cried. "Donna Bruce was murdered?!"

"Didn't we already establish that?" asked Chase with a frown.

"Murdered!" muttered the producer, staring before him. Then a keen look came into his eyes. "So that's why you're here, bugging me with all these questions." He thought for a moment. "If I were you, I'd take a long, hard look at the husband. Tad Rip. He was the main reason Donna pulled out of *A Star is Born*. Wanted his wife all to himself. Jealous of her career and jealous as hell of her co-stars."

"So jealous he forced her to stop acting?" asked Chase.

"Pretty much. Couldn't handle his wife being more successful than him, I guess."

Odelia shared a look with Chase. This was the second person who'd pointed at Tad Rip as a potential suspect.

"Did anyone see you on your porch this morning at seven, Mr. Montlló?" asked Chase.

"Of course."

"Who?"

The man gestured at his dog. "Flea saw me. And he's as honest as can be."

Chase grimaced. "I'm afraid I'm going to need a human witness, sir."

The man gestured around. "Ask anybody. They'll all vouch for me. I never leave this porch. Heck, I almost live on this porch these days."

"Don't you have any plans to return to the movie business?" asked Odelia.

The man smiled a crooked smile. "Oh, I've got plenty of plans, honey, but no money to back them up. And ever since the Donna Bruce thing no friends to help me out, either." He patted Flea's back. "Except for Flea here. He's been my loyal companion for years. Wouldn't dream of deserting me, would you, old buddy?"

The dog barked once, acknowledging his master's words. For an ex-green beret, Ransom Montlló looked pretty harmless, Odelia decided. And what was more, he hardly looked capable of carrying out such a sophisticated murder. Stealing and transporting a beehive, breaking into Donna's house, locking her into her sauna and siccing the bees on her? Not exactly his cup of tea.

Chase seemed to feel the same way, for he thanked Mr. Montlló for his time, and then they were off.

"I don't think he did it," Chase intimated as they returned to their cars.

"I don't think so either. And if he wanted to kill Donna, he would have done it years ago. And not way out here in the middle of nowhere with his brown paper bag and his dog called Flea."

They looked back at the boarding house and Ransom gave them a wave. Odelia waved back. No, he looked harmless enough, she reckoned.

"Sad story, though. To be on top of the world one minute and down in the dumps the next."

"Yeah, almost like the story of *A Star is Born*," Chase said. "Donna Bruce went on to become a big star with her website, while her mentor became a washout."

"Ransom was her mentor?"

"Sure. Ransom Montlló was the man who gave Donna Bruce her very first shot at fame and stardom. He cast her in her breakout role. A prostitute with a heart of gold who gets involved with an honest man who tries to get her out of that racket."

"The remake of *Pretty Woman*?"

"No. The remake of *Irma la Douce*. Though I prefer the original."

"Of course you do. So what's next?" she asked, leaning against her car.

"Now we talk to the ex-husband." He tapped the side of his nose. "And if my intuition is right, he just might be our guy."

CHAPTER 13

*I*t took us a long time to find out anything from the Internet. Cats aren't exactly equipped to work on computers. For one thing, we don't come outfitted with a set of digits that make for good typing, and if you use your claws it's easy to totally wreck a regular computer keyboard. So Harriet tried to use her paw pads, but that proved really hit and miss. And we were just about to give up, when Dooley saw a picture of a nice kitty on the screen and touched it with his paw.

"Don't touch the screen!" I yelled, but too late. And then the small picture of the kitty suddenly blew up into a big picture of the same kitty and we all stared at it.

"What just happened?" asked Brutus.

"I don't know," said Dooley. "I touched the screen and something changed."

"Do it again," Harriet urged.

So Dooley touched the screen again, careful not to use his claws, and the screen changed again, this time to a set of pictures of the same kitty posing up a storm. "So weird," he said, staring from his paws to the screen. "Do you think I have magical paws? That must be it, right? I must have magical paws." A look of absolute delight came over his face. "Imagine what I can do with my magical paws! Maybe everything I touch changes into something else!" And to try out this new theory of his, he immediately touched Harriet's face.

"Hey!" she yelled, slapping his paw away. "What do you think you're doing?"

"I just wanted to change your frown into a smile," he said sheepishly.

Harriet's frown only deepened, debunking Dooley's magical paws theory.

Meanwhile, Brutus had also put his big paw on the screen. Nothing happened and he growled with annoyance. "Stupid screen," he grumbled.

"I think it's one of those touchscreens," I said, a memory stirring in the back of my mind. The computer Odelia had set up for us was her old work computer, and I seemed to remember her once telling me something about it being one of the first models with a touchscreen. Since I had no idea at the time what a touchscreen was, I hadn't really paid any attention to her words, but now it dawned on me. You touch the screen, and something happens!

"Touch that kitty," I told Brutus.

"You're not touching that kitty," Harriet said when Brutus made to follow my instructions.

"But it's not a real kitty," he said now.

"I don't care. You are not touching that kitty, Brutus, and that's my final word!"

"So you touch that kitty," I suggested.

"What? Eww! I'm not that kind of cat, Max."

I groaned. "Okay, so I'll touch the kitty."

"Can I touch the kitty?" Dooley asked. "I like touching kitties."

That much was obvious. Dooley placed his 'magical' paw on the kitty's face and suddenly it morphed into a 'bio' page, which told us the kitty's name was Susan and she possessed a sweet and disarming personality. She also liked taking long naps on the couch and chasing her own tail.

"*I* like chasing my own tail!" Dooley exclaimed. "Looks like me and Susan are a match made in heaven." And since he was having so much fun, he kept on putting his paw on the screen, scrolling down the page to read more about Susan's daring and exciting habits.

We watched the phenomenon with fascination, and for the next five minutes found out everything there was to know about Susan, including her love of belly rubs. Only when Harriet had finally wrested back control over the computer, she managed to steer the Internet search in the right direction again. Half an hour later we were up to date on Donna Bruce, thanks to the power of the touchscreen and the tendency of the Internet to remember everything about everyone. Turned out Donna used to have a boyfriend, something even Odelia probably didn't know. His name was Dexter Valdès and he was the spitting image of Ricky Martin, only about two decades younger. For some strange reason, all the pictures we could find featured Dexter with naked torso, though that could have been Harriet, of course.

"It says here they broke up," she said, having found a site called TMZ. "It also says Dexter felt emasculated in his boy toy role, especially after Donna wrote a blog post on donna.vip about him and his tiny wiener." She looked up. "What is a wiener?"

"It's a kind of sausage," I said knowingly. "Some people really like it."

"I like sausage," Brutus grunted.

"Me too," Dooley chimed in.

"Me too," I said with a wistful sigh. No more wieners for

me in the near future, though. Odelia had already tucked my usual kibble away in a safe place where I couldn't find it, and replaced it with the special diet kind that tasted like cardboard. From now on, and until the scale dipped below what Vena had determined was my ideal body weight, it was the only food I was going to get, and no more than one bowl of the filthy stuff either.

Brutus gave me a smirk. "No more wieners for you, huh, Max?"

I scowled at him. "You don't have to rub it in."

"I believe I will," he said. "You always told me your bulk was all muscle. Well, as it turns out that was a big, fat lie. It's all flab, just like I thought."

"It's not flab. It is muscle. I just have too much of it is all."

"You can't have too much muscle," he said, flexing his shoulder muscles. "No, just admit it, Max. You are one flabby tabby."

Dooley laughed at this, but when I turned my scowl on him, he quickly stopped.

"Guys," said Harriet urgently. "I don't think Donna was referring to Dexter's sausage after all. Her blog post was all about his... performance."

I noticed her ears had taken on a reddish tinge, and her eyes were glittering brightly. "Performance? What performance?" I asked. Anything was better than to have to listen to Brutus's taunts about my 'bulk.'

"I think she was referring to his... sexual performance," she said. She then turned to us, eyes wide. "I think a wiener is... a pee-pee."

Now we were all staring at the screen, eagerly drinking in the details of Donna Bruce's blog post. I'm not a great reader, but it soon became clear to me that the article was a lot more revealing than any human male would have appreciated. Not only was there a lot of talk about Dexter's pee-pee and its lack of size and performance, there was also a long bit about his endurance or lack thereof. All in all, the piece wasn't entirely flattering to Donna's boy toy, and I could understand why the two of them hadn't been a couple at the time of Donna's untimely demise.

"But why would she write all that?" I asked. "That's just a lot of very private stuff."

"Some people are like that," said Harriet knowingly. "They just enjoy sharing all of their private things with the world."

"Judging from that TMZ article Dexter didn't agree."

"No, it must have hurt his chances with other females," said Brutus. "No woman likes a guy with a small pee-pee." When I frowned at him, he quickly added, "At least that's what I'm guessing. Personally I have no problem in that department."

Harriet gave him a small smile. "No, you definitely don't."

"Size matters," said Dooley knowingly, and we all turned to him. "It does," he said defensively. "The bigger the sausage the more meat. And we all like meat, don't we?"

I slapped my brow. "Dooley, do you still think Donna was writing about meat?"

"Of course she was. A wiener is a kind of sausage. That's what you just said."

"It's also a pee-pee," I said. "Which is what Harriet just said."

"What is a pee-pee?" asked Dooley with a frown.

Harriet groaned. "Oh, Dooley."

CHAPTER 14

*O*delia and Chase found Tad Rip, the illustrious ex-husband of whom they'd heard so much by now, presiding over lunch while a nanny had a hard time keeping his two boys in check. Sweetums and Honeychild turned out to be six-year-old twins, and quite a handful. Mr. Rip himself appeared distraught when Odelia and Chase were led out onto the patio by an assistant. The house where he lived was still under construction, as bare bulbs dangled from the concrete ceiling and boxes stood piled up all over the place.

"Don't mind the mess," said Tad, who looked like a million bucks in a power suit and a stylish pair of expensive sunglasses. "I just moved in last week." He gave them an apologetic grimace. "Great timing, as it turns out."

"Our condolences for your loss," said Odelia as she took the proffered seat at the table.

"Thanks. Donna and I were divorced but she was still the mother of my boys. Cut it out, will you!" he hollered at the two rascals, who were hitting their nanny with super soakers. The girl screamed, trying to evade the twin beams of water.

"I didn't know the kids were with you," said Chase, looking out across the immaculately landscaped garden. At least that part of the house was ready. "It was my understanding that Mrs. Bruce had sole custody and denied you visitation rights?"

"She did," said Tad as he removed his sunglasses and rubbed his eyes. "But lately we'd become civil with each other again. We were even on speaking terms—we just talked last night, actually, mainly about the boys' future. Our divorce might have been acrimonious but for the sake of Sweetums and Honeychild we decided to put our differences aside and work things out. Which is why I moved back out here—to be closer to the boys. I was going to have them every weekend while they spent the week with their mother."

"What's going to happen now?" asked Odelia.

The man shrugged, and she noticed the bags under his eyes. "No idea. I guess I'll have them full-time from now on. Not what I was counting on but I'll manage. I'll have to."

They stared out at the kids, who were now chasing the nanny around the yard. "They seem to have taken the news pretty well," said Chase.

"It hasn't sunk in yet. I told them this morning what happened—that their mommy now lives with the angels in heaven, looking down on them from up above. They thought that was pretty cool. Like Superwoman. I guess it'll take them some time to come to terms with the whole thing."

"I'm sorry to have to ask you this, Mr. Rip," said Odelia, "but where were you this morning between seven and eight?"

"You can ask me anything you want. I just hope you catch whoever did this before they strike again. I was trying to wake up the kids. We were going to church and I needed them to get ready."

"Is there anyone who can vouch for you?" asked Chase.

"Sure. Elsie was here—that's the nanny. And Germaine—the housekeeper. Oh, and you just met Herman—he's my executive assistant. And then there's the executive protection detail—Franz and Hans. They guard the boys twenty-four seven."

"They all live here?" asked Odelia.

"Yeah, they do. There's also Arnold—the driver—but he doesn't live on-site."

"And they were all here with you when Mrs. Bruce was killed," Chase said, just to make sure.

"Yeah, they were. A man in my position is rarely alone. I can't afford to be. I've got a billion-dollar company to run and now I've got a family to think about as well. A lot of moving parts so any helping hand is more than welcome."

"Do you have any idea who might be behind the murder of your ex-wife, sir?" asked Odelia.

The man frowned and rubbed his jaw. "Well, if I had to venture a guess, I'd take a long, hard look at Dexter. That's Dexter Valdès. He was Donna's boyfriend for a couple of years, though they broke up not so long ago. Dexter has had a few bad things to say about Donna, especially after she wrote that article about him on her site. I guess he didn't take it too well."

"Why? What happened?"

The business tycoon smiled. "Donna liked to live her life out in the open—for the world to see. She held nothing back, which was one of the reasons our marriage failed. I can't afford to have every minute of every day shared with the rest of the world. If you're a businessman you can't operate like that. My competitors would have a field day if they could anticipate my next move. But Donna was a relentless marketer of her own life. She turned oversharing into a form of art. So when she decided to share with the world what happened between the sheets with Dexter, the guy wasn't too happy about it, especially since he didn't come out smelling of roses."

"What do you mean?"

The man's smile widened. "I don't remember all the details, but there was a piece about the man's tiny wiener that went viral, inspiring lots of memes, if that's the term. Suffice it to say Dexter left in a huff, claiming she'd caused irreparable damage to his reputation. Which she probably had. Not that she cared one bit. Donna was self-centered that way. She didn't care who she hurt in her relentless pursuit of fame and fortune."

"You sound bitter," Odelia remarked.

"I do? Well, maybe I was bitter—for a long time." He glanced at Sweetums and Honeychild, who'd now resorted to turning the super soakers on each other and were screeching up a storm. "But when I look at what she gave me, my bitterness fades. Donna Bruce was a complicated woman, detectives, but she did at least one thing right: she was a loving mother."

"Did she also share every minute of every day of the twins' lives online?" asked Chase.

"No, she did not. Oddly enough that's where she drew the line. Said the boys got to decide for themselves if they wanted to lead the kind of life she did, and as long as they were underage, she would protect their privacy with the fierceness of a lioness. Which she did."

CHAPTER 15

Frankly I was growing a little tired of Harriet's Internet search as the be-all and end-all of sleuthing, so when she started getting engrossed in an article about Blac Chyna, claiming it was giving her valuable insight into the celebrity mindset, I decided to bail out. Dooley, who'd grown as bored with the whole Internet sleuthing thing as I had, tagged along. Harriet may have been in charge of this investigation, but so far she hadn't really uncovered all that much. We now knew Beyoncé's twins Rumi and Sir Carter were teething, the *Real Housewives of New York* really didn't get along, and the *Duck Dynasty* men had shaved their beards for some charity event. What we still didn't know was the identity of Donna Bruce's murderer.

And as we ambled along the street, we decided to go old school on this thing again: visit our usual haunts and interrogate every cat in town about what they knew and what they'd seen and heard. We wouldn't get the latest intel on Justin Bieber, *Duck Dynasty,* or Blac Chyna, whoever they might be, but we might finally solve this murder case.

"Brutus was awfully quiet just now," said Dooley. "Do you think he's sick?"

"He's henpecked is what he is," I said.

"Henpecked? But he's not a hen."

"It's just an expression. It means Harriet is now firmly in charge of his life."

"Oh." Dooley thought about this for a moment. "So that's a good thing, right?"

"I guess so." It hadn't stopped him from bullyragging me about my diet, though, so the extent of his henpeckedness was still an open question. My money was definitely on Harriet, though. If anyone could get Brutus to toe the line, it was her.

Our first stop was the doctor's office, where I hoped to exchange a few words with Gran. By now she was probably ensconced behind her trusty front desk, encouraging patients waiting for a medical tête-à-tête with Odelia's dad to sit down and be quiet, so now might be a good time to ask her what she thought about Donna and what the word on the street was.

We waltzed into the waiting room, which was empty, and headed straight for Gran. She was deeply engrossed in Donna Magazine, probably picking out what else she could buy from the site. She started when we showed up behind her, and Dooley caroled out a blithe, "Hey, Gran!"

Pressing a hand to her heart, she cried, "You scared me! Creeping up on me like that."

"Sorry about that," said Dooley. "We just thought we'd pay you a visit."

"Actually we wanted to find out if you'd heard anything about the Donna Bruce case," I said. "You know. Some new scuttlebutt or something."

"Yeah, Odelia put Harriet in charge of the investigation

but all she does is read stories about Justin Bieber on the Internet," Dooley explained.

"I haven't heard anything, to be honest," said Gran thoughtfully. "People don't really seem to be tuned into the whole Donna Bruce drama." She shrugged her bony shoulders. "I guess Donna was an acquired taste—more for the discerning cognoscenti like me." She tapped her glossy magazine, which was open on an article extolling the healing power of crystals. Gran leaned down and dropped her voice to a whisper. "Has another package arrived by any chance?"

We both shook our heads. "Nope," I said.

Gran's lips tightened into an expression of disapproval. "They promised me it would arrive today."

"But you already had two packages today," I reminded her.

"So? Three's the charm. This third package is the bee's knees. The absolute cream of the crop. It's a…" She hesitated, taking in our curious expressions. Then she shook her head. "I'd better not tell you. This is for adults only."

"But we are adults," said Dooley. "I'm four, which in human years is…" He thought hard, but finally had to give up.

"You're still too young," said Gran. "I don't want to spoil your innocence. Odelia would never forgive me. Which reminds me—when a new package arrives, can you let me know right away? Odelia doesn't even have to know about it."

"Sure," I said. "We'll be your eyes and ears, Gran."

She smiled. "I will make it worth your while." She opened a desk drawer and took out a small packet of Cat Snax, tore it open and distributed its contents on the floor.

"Oh, gee, Gran!" I cried, digging in with relish. "How did you know these are my favorite?!"

Her smile widened. "Grandmothers know these things,

Max. And if you keep me informed about the UPS guy arriving, there's a lot more where this came from."

"But he's not supposed to," said Dooley. "Max, you're not supposed to. You're on a diet."

"Diet schmiet," said Gran. "You only live once, Max. So you better enjoy it while you can."

"My kind of woman," I said, swallowing down some more of the tasty treats.

"But he's too fat!" Dooley cried. "Vena said he's going to get heart ar—arithmetic."

"Arrhythmia?" asked Gran. "Don't listen to doctors, Dooley. They'll only try to scare you into giving up the best things in life. Take me for example. Tex has been telling me for years I shouldn't drink coffee. That it's bad for me. Well, no doctor in the world is going to make me give up coffee." And to show us she meant business, she took a sip from her cup of coffee, slurping loudly and smacking her lips with relish. "You just enjoy your Cat Snax, Max," she said, "and don't let that nasty Vena take them away from you."

I looked up, having devoured the entire packet. "Thanks, Gran. I think you just graduated to being my favorite person on the planet."

"You can't do that," said Dooley, alarmed. "She's my favorite person on the planet."

"She can be both our favorite person on the planet," I told him.

"She can?" he asked, surprised.

"Sure. There's no limit on how many people's favorite person you can be."

"Oh, crap," Gran suddenly said, looking up in alarm. When I saw Odelia peeking down at us from across the counter, I knew we were in trouble. Big trouble.

CHAPTER 16

"*M*ax! Gran!" Odelia didn't know who she should be mad at more: Gran for providing Max with these sugary snacks that would ruin his diet, or Max for accepting and eating them.

"I was giving him what he needs," said Gran snappishly. "You can't expect him to subsist on such a crappy diet."

"He's too fat. He has to go on a diet," she said. "If he doesn't, he might get all kinds of diseases."

"Says who?"

"Says Vena!"

Gran waved a deprecating hand. "Who listens to stupid doctors?"

"I do—you do—we all do!"

"Not me. Uh-uh. If I'd listened to your father I'd have stopped working a long time ago, and would be sitting at home crocheting. He seems to think that a woman my age has no business being out and about and enjoying life to the fullest."

"That's not true and you know it. Dad was the one who

told you to work past your retirement. He said you're way too active to sit at home and do nothing."

"Look, Max is my baby and if I can't even spoil my babies…"

Odelia's eye fell on the copy of Donna Magazine. "Don't tell me you've been ordering more of that Donna junk." When her grandmother didn't respond, she cried, "Gran!"

"What? I need this stuff. I need all of it!"

"You don't need any of it. If Dad knew you've been ordering online again, he'd cut up his credit cards and make sure you never get near a computer again."

"Well, he won't know if you won't tell him, will he?"

Just at that moment, the door to Dad's office opened and Tex Poole himself walked out. Dad was a big and bluff man, well-liked and respected by the Hampton Cove community. He was also a great doctor. "What's going on here?" he asked. "I thought a fight had broken out or something."

"A fight has broken out," Odelia assured him. "Gran has been giving Max Cat Snax."

"Oh?" asked Dad. "And that's bad because…"

"Because Max is on a diet. He's not supposed to eat anything other than the diet kibble Vena has prescribed him."

"Right," Dad said. "Of course." He wagged a dutiful finger in Gran's face. "Only diet food from now on, Vesta. No more Cat Snax for Max."

"But he loves his Cat Snax," said Gran. "And look at him. He's not fat. He's just the right size for his body type." To prove her point, she tried to pick Max up from the floor and deposit him on her desk. Unfortunately, the ginger cat proved too heavy and she couldn't manage. "That doesn't mean a thing," she said defiantly.

Dad stepped into the breach and picked Max up and studied him. The way he was dangling from Dad's large hands, his hind paws stretched out and his face a mask of annoyance, it appeared the ginger tabby wasn't too happy to be handled like this.

"He is a bit on the heavy side," Dad agreed. "And he could definitely use some more exercise."

At this, Max's eyes went wide. "Exercise?" he cried. "I don't need no stinkin' exercise!"

"Maybe you're right, Dad," said Odelia. "If he's not going to follow his diet, maybe we should just make sure he's more active. Maybe I should take him to the gym with me from now on. Make him run on the treadmill. A couple of miles a day would do the trick."

"Not the treadmill!" Max cried. "I hate the treadmill!"

"They sell special cat treadmills nowadays," said Dad. "It's more like a big hamster wheel, built for cats, but it'll do the trick."

"But I'm not a hamster!" Max yelled, still dangling from Dad's hands. "Please—I'll be good. I won't eat Cat Snax anymore. I'll stick to my diet from now on."

"Or maybe you could just take him for a walk every day," Dad continued. "You could buy him one of those leashes—like the ones they use for dogs—and you walk him twice a day. That should take care of that excess weight."

Odelia thought about this. "You know, Dad?" she finally said. "That might not be such a bad idea."

"No! I'll be good! I'll eat that diet crap—I mean that diet food!"

"Or I could do both," said Odelia. "I could feed him the diet kibble *and* take him for a walk every day." She nodded, her mind made up. "It's good for you, Max, and it will speed up your weight loss. Kickstart it." She ignored the look of panic in the cat's eyes. "And who knows, if you lose those pounds fast enough, I might even let you have some Cat Snax from time to time."

"I just think you're torturing the poor creature," said Gran disdainfully.

"And as for you," Odelia said, turning to her grandmother, "no more ordering stuff online. Is that understood?"

"Has she been ordering online again?" asked Dad, surprised.

"Loads of stuff. She's been shipping it to my address." Gran darted a quick look in Max's direction and Odelia saw what was going on here. A secret alliance between cat and human. No more, though. She wasn't going to condone this kind of subterfuge. "Dad, I think you better cancel your credit cards."

Gran looked horrified. "You can't do that!"

"Oh, but I can," Dad assured her. "And I probably should." He seemed to waver for a moment. "Of course, it's a whole hassle to apply for new credit cards. Maybe if you promise me that from now on you'll behave, I won't have to take such a drastic step."

Gran nodded anxiously. "I promise! From now on, no more ordering online!"

"Dad, don't fall for those empty promises. You know she'll break them the first chance she gets."

"Well, I for one believe her," said Dad.

"You're a good man, Tex," said Gran. "And an ever better son-in-law. I just knew I was doing the right thing when I advised Marge to marry you and not that bum Jock Farnsworth."

Dad frowned at this. "Vesta," he warned.

"Well, that's what happened! Good thing I told Marge to pick you." She gave Dad a radiant smile.

Odelia looked from Gran to her dad. "Who is Jock Farnsworth?"

"Nobody," said Dad quickly, throwing Gran a dark look.

"He was your mother's boyfriend around the time she was dating your father," said Gran.

"Mom was dating two guys at the same time?"

"Can you imagine?" Gran chuckled. "Your mother was quite the hot chick. She had so many suitors we had to fight them off with a stick, your grandpa and me. But when she told me she couldn't decide between Jock and Tex, I was the one who made her pick Tex."

Dad rolled his eyes. He was obviously not happy with Gran raking up this ancient family history. Odelia narrowed her eyes at Dad. So that's why he was so easy on Gran using his credit card. She was holding this Jock Farnsworth over his head.

"Who's Jock Farnsworth?" she asked again.

"Nobody!" Dad insisted.

"Franklin Farnsworth's kid," said Gran.

"Franklin Farnsworth? The chicken wing guy? The richest man in Hampton Cove?

"He's not that rich," Dad muttered darkly.

"He is super rich," Gran said with a smirk. "And now Jock's poised to step into his father's shoes and take over the family business, *he'll* be the richest man in town. And he could have been your daddy, Odelia."

She stared at her grandmother. It was hard to believe Mom had dated Franklin Farnsworth's son once upon a time. Talk about ghosts from the past.

"Are we done talking about Jock Farnsworth?" asked Dad irritably.

"Sure, whatever you say, Tex," said Gran, still that smirk on her face. She had Dad just where she wanted him and she knew it.

"What happened to Jock?" asked Odelia. "After Mom broke up with him, I mean."

"Well, let me see," said Gran, pretending to think hard.

"Oh, that's right. He married Grace Carpenter—Ralph Carpenter's only daughter."

"Ralph Carpenter. The second richest man in town."

"Sure. Ralph and Franklin always dreamed of joining their families. Marge breaking up with Jock paved the way."

So not only had Mom dated the richest kid in Hampton Cove, but now that kid was married to the richest girl in town. And no one had ever told her! Dad was still scowling at Gran, so she patted his shoulder. "Mom made the right decision, Dad," she assured him.

"You think so?" he asked, not seeming convinced.

"She married my dad, didn't she?"

Dad smiled and gave her a hug. "Thanks, honey. That's very sweet of you."

"Franklin Farnsworth was bad news anyway," said Gran. "Imagine Marge marrying into that family and spending every holiday at Farnsworth Castle, having to be nice to Irma Farnsworth." She shivered. "We had a narrow escape there, Tex."

"We sure did," said Dad softly.

Odelia wanted to know more about these secrets from her family's past, but both Tex and Gran were eager to change the topic, so she decided to leave it at that. She'd just ask Mom instead.

"Actually the reason I dropped by was to ask you about Donna Bruce," Odelia told her dad.

"Oh, right. The murder case. Terrible business, that. Simply terrible."

"Was she a patient of yours?"

"No, she wasn't. She used a concierge doctor. Though I knew of her, of course. Before she became a lifestyle tycoon she was a wonderful actress."

"The bee stings," said Odelia. "I always thought bee stings weren't lethal?"

"Well, they can be if you get enough of them," said Tex. "And then there's the fact that some people are allergic and can go into anaphylactic shock. I guess Donna was one of those people."

"I don't think so," said Odelia. "The coroner would have mentioned it in his report. The cause of death was definitely the bee stings. She apparently suffered thousands of them in a very short amount of time."

"That would do it," said Dad. "The average person can tolerate ten stings per pound of body weight. So she must have sustained a lot of them."

"But could she have survived the attack?"

"Very unlikely," said Dad. "From what I understand, thousands of bees were unleashed on the poor woman. And the fact that she was in the sauna, with nothing to protect her, means she would have suffered stings all over her body. Whoever planned this must have thought things through."

Gran was shaking her head. "Who could have done such a terrible thing?"

"Well, as it turns out Donna Bruce made a lot of enemies over the years," said Odelia. "She was not a well-liked woman."

"I can see that," said Dad, nodding. "She had a reputation for being difficult and demanding."

"I hope you catch the culprit, honey," said Gran. "Donna was my hero. I wouldn't know what to do without some of the stuff she advised on her website."

Odelia remembered the jade eggs and thought Gran could have done without them with no trouble at all. Then again, maybe Dad was right. If Gran really wanted to buy all this stuff, and he didn't mind funding her Donna fixation, who was she to stop her?

Picking up her two cats, she left the doctor's office and set foot for the police station. She was meeting with her uncle and Chase to discuss the case and this time she wanted Max and Dooley to be present when she did. Chase might think it a little strange when she brought two cats to the meeting but so be it. He would just have to get used to the fact that she was a crazy cat lady, as he'd told her on more than one occasion.

CHAPTER 17

"So how did your sleuthing session with Harriet and Brutus go?" she asked as they were walking down the street, en route to the police station.

"Terrible," Max sighed. "We now know everything about Justin Bieber's tattoos and Blac Chyna's favorite designers. We even know how many nannies Rumi and Sir Carter have—"

"Rumi and Sir Carter?"

"Beyoncé and Jay-Z's twins," said Dooley knowingly. "They're very cute."

"—but we still don't know a thing about who killed Donna Bruce," Max finished. "Oh, but we did find out she had a boyfriend with a tiny wee-wee. His name is—"

"Dexter Valdès. Yes, Donna's ex-husband told us about him. He looks like a great suspect."

"What about the ex-husband?" asked Max. "I thought he did it?"

"He has a solid alibi. He was with the boys. Sweetums and Honeychild."

"Of course he was."

Odelia looked down, noticing that Max's breath was a little labored. "Are you all right down there, honey? Do you want me to carry you?"

"No, I'm fine," said Max, holding up a paw. "Never felt better."

But judging from the way he walked, he was having trouble with his weight. He lumbered, his step not as graceful as it used to be. It frankly worried her. "Don't eat Cat Snax anymore, Max," she urged. "That stuff's full of sugar. It's not good for you."

"I know," he said. "It's just that I'm hungry all the time."

"Drink more water," Dooley advised. "Whenever I'm hungry and I don't feel like eating, I just drink a lot of water —really fill up my tummy. And then I'm not hungry anymore."

"That's the worst advice I've ever heard," Max grumbled. "Drink more water. I'm hungry, Dooley, not thirsty."

"But if your stomach is full, you won't be hungry. And water doesn't have any calories, or does it?"

"No, it doesn't," Odelia assured him. "Listen to Dooley, Max. Whenever you get hungry, just drink more. Maybe you'll be able to handle your cravings that way."

Max gave her a dubious look. It was obvious he wasn't buying it.

They arrived at the police station and she entered, holding the door for the cats. Usually the feline duo snuck around the back and lounged on Chief Alec's windowsill. Today she wanted them to be present in the room, though. She hoped they could help find out what was going on.

"Hey, I don't think we were ever in here," said Dooley, looking around excitedly.

"Yeah, almost like being invited to visit the Queen of England," said Max.

They passed Dolores and set foot for her uncle's office.

She entered without knocking, as usual, and took a seat across the desk from the Chief, who sat discussing the case with Chase.

"I see you brought your feline little friends," said Uncle Alec amiably as he glanced down at Max and Dooley. "To what do I owe the pleasure?"

"I found them wandering down the street and figured I'd better take them along, in case they got lost again," she said.

Uncle Alec nodded. He'd gotten the message. Chase, however, seemed surprised. "You're awfully protective of those cats, aren't you? Can't they find their own way home? I always thought cats had some kind of homing instinct?"

"They do," said Odelia, "but Max has been having some medical issues. He needs to be watched closely."

"Medical issues, huh?" asked Max with an offended look at Odelia. "So now all of a sudden I'm an invalid? Thanks for nothing."

She smiled down at the spreading ginger cat. "You're welcome, Max."

"Mh? What was that?" asked Chase.

"Oh, I was just talking to myself."

"She does that a lot," Uncle Alec explained. "Even as a child she was always talking to herself. Drove us crazy."

"Did she now?" asked Chase, darting a curious look down at Max and Dooley.

"So what did your dad have to say?" asked Uncle Alec, getting down to business.

"He said that whoever murdered Donna knew what they were doing. They used enough bees to make sure the attack would be deadly, even if Donna proved not to be allergic to bee stings."

"So we're dealing with a professional," Chase grunted. "First time I've ever heard of bees being used as a murder weapon."

"People underestimate how many bees it takes to kill a person," said Odelia. "Stings from bees might be very painful, but they are rarely deadly."

"So do you think we should look at beekeepers?" asked Chase.

"I doubt it," said Uncle Alec. "No beekeeper would sacrifice his precious bees for this kind of thing. It's hard enough to keep them alive, with bees dying out at a troubling rate and beekeepers losing large percentages of their hives. It's a huge investment in both monetary terms and time-wise."

"So we're looking for someone who wanted Donna dead and knew a thing or two about bees."

"Stands to reason that the person who stole the hives would have suffered a few bee stings in the process," Uncle Alec said thoughtfully. "So that's one other thing to look into."

"What about the boyfriend?" asked Odelia. "Any sign of this Dexter Valdès yet?"

"So far nothing," said Uncle Alec. "We did find out he still lives in town, but he wasn't home when we sent some officers by to pick him up. But don't worry. We'll find him soon enough. I put out an APB for his arrest."

Just then, there was a loud altercation in the hallway, and when Odelia got up to take a closer look, she saw that two officers were bringing in a handsome-looking man who was the spitting image of Ricky Martin, only two decades younger. He was handcuffed and shouting at the officers.

"Dexter Valdès," said one of the officers, panting slightly from the exertion of subduing the man. "We picked him up at Pier's Pont. Bar fight."

"I hate Donna!" the man suddenly screamed at the top of his lungs. "I hate Donna and I'm glad she's dead!"

CHAPTER 18

It was the first time we got to sit in on a police interrogation and I was adamant to make the most of it. I was hungry, though, so first I needed a snack. So when no one was watching, I snuck into Chief Alec's office and quickly found what I was looking for. While I was in there before I'd noticed the chief kept a half-eaten meatball sub in his bottom drawer. The scent had been driving me crazy.

"Max! What are you doing?!" Dooley shouted from the door.

"I'm foraging! What does it look like I'm doing?!"

"But you can't! You promised Odelia you would stick to your diet!"

"I lied, okay? I can't stand it anymore, Dooley. I'm not like you. I can't fill my stomach with water and pretend I'm not hungry! I'm starving!"

So I skewered the meatball from between the two buns with one nail and popped it into my mouth. Yummy. Then I went looking for a second meatball, which I hoped was in there somewhere.

"Max! Someone's coming!" Dooley suddenly yelled. "Too late!"

"What are you guys doing in here?" asked Odelia, entering the office at a trot. She picked up a file from the desk and glanced down at me. She took one look at the meatball sub—now sans meatball—and her brows knitted into a frown. "Max! You're cheating on your diet again!"

"No, I'm not," I said.

She planted a hand on her hip. "I can see the sauce dripping from your lips, Max."

Oops. I quickly swiped my tongue along my lips. "There. All gone," I said, then burped.

She shook her head. "Oh, Max. What am I going to do with you?"

"I told him he shouldn't!" Dooley said.

"Tattletale!" I hissed.

"Come on, you two," said Odelia. "We don't have time for this. We're about to interrogate Dexter Valdès."

She ushered us out of the office and closed the door. I could have told her this wasn't necessary, as I'd already determined there wasn't a second meatball inside that sub. Uncle Alec must have dug it out and eaten it himself.

We followed Odelia down the corridor and then into a small room, where a mirror offered a view of a second, even smaller room. We hopped up on the table at Chief Alec's instigation and made ourselves comfortable while Odelia joined Chase in the next room and sat down across from Dexter Valdès. In my personal opinion the man only barely resembled Ricky Martin. His eyes were bloodshot, his cheeks stubbled and his hair unkempt. He might have been younger, but right now he looked like a much seedier and disheveled version of the fabled Latino heartthrob and hit sensation.

"So, Dexter," said Chase, opening the proceedings, "you hate Donna Bruce so much you're happy she's dead, huh?"

The man seemed a lot less vocal about his hatred of Donna Bruce than before. He gave Chase a wary look. "Look, dude, when I said that I didn't really mean it."

"Oh, backpedaling are we?"

"You had a fight at Pier's Pont just now," said Odelia. "When the owner called the police you were trying to shove a billiard ball down the throat of another patron, telling him your wiener was the biggest wiener in wiener history. Is that correct?"

Dexter nodded. "That sounds about right. In my defense, he made fun of my wiener."

"Could this be related to the article Donna wrote about your wiener?" asked Chase.

"It's got everything to do with that article," Dexter confessed. "If she hadn't written that article my life wouldn't have turned into a vaudeville act. Now everyone is making fun of my wiener. I haven't even had a girlfriend in months, all because of that damn article."

"So you did hate Donna Bruce, and you did want to kill her," said Chase.

The man threw up his arms. "How would you feel when someone shared the size of your wiener with the world, dude?"

"I'd feel comfortable enough in my own skin not to let it bother me," said Chase.

"Bullshit. No man likes to have his wiener become the butt of a joke. I suffered, all right? And that's just what she wanted. My wiener isn't tiny. At least not as tiny as she made it out to be. My wiener is just fine. In fact my wiener is nothing short of majestic and I can prove it." He got up and started removing his pants, which was a little hard to do with the handcuffs restricting his movements. Chase pushed him down in his seat again.

"Sit down, buddy," the burly cop said. "I'm not interested

in the size of your junk. All I want is for you to tell me where you got those bees and how you got them into Donna's house."

The man's eyes widened. "Bees? What are you talking about?"

"You stole those bees and then you transported them to Donna's house. How did you know how to handle them?"

"But I don't know anything about bees." Then understanding seemed to dawn on him. "Oh, you think I killed Donna? With bees? Are you nuts?"

"No, but I think you are if you're going to claim you're innocent. You practically confessed to murdering your ex-girlfriend. Now all we need to establish is how you did it."

"But I didn't kill her!"

"You just told us you did!"

"No, I didn't! I just said I'm happy she's dead. I would never hurt anyone—least of all Donna. She might have written all that stuff about my wiener but I genuinely liked her. We had a great time together." He squinched his eyes closed. "Look, dude. I say a lot of dumb shit, but that doesn't mean I mean any of it."

"Then tell me where you were at seven this morning, when Donna was murdered."

"At Pier's Pont, of course, where you guys picked me up."

"You expect me to believe you hang around at bars at such an early hour?"

"No, I expect you to believe I hang around at bars at such a late hour. I'd been there all night. Just ask Johnny, the bartender. He knows my face. I'm a regular."

"Johnny Dusky," Chase muttered, checking his notes. "That would be the guy who called in the altercation."

"Yeah, I think he got annoyed when I started rearranging the furniture," Dexter said with a grin.

Dooley gave me a nudge. "Looks like the guy didn't do it, Max."

"Looks like you're right," I agreed. "Another dead end, huh?"

"We seem to be running into a lot of dead ends lately, Max. Do you think we're losing our touch?"

"It's this diet. It's making me feel weak. I can't think straight when I'm hungry, and I'm hungry all the time."

"You just had a giant meatball!"

"Just the one, though. I could eat ten giant meatballs and still feel hungry."

Just then, two more cats joined us. They were Harriet and Brutus.

"You guys!" Harriet yelled, gracefully jumping up on the desk. "I know who killed Donna!"

"You do?" I asked.

"She does," said Brutus proudly, also joining us. "We figured it out together, didn't we, sugar pie?"

"We sure did, scrunchy munch."

"So?" asked Dooley. "Who did it?"

"Maureen Cranberry!"

Dooley and I exchanged a puzzled glance. "Who's Maureen Cranberry?" I asked.

"She's a woman who filed charges against Donna Bruce for burning her... you know."

Curiouser and curiouser. "No, I don't. Burning her what?"

She leaned in, and faux-whispered, "Her business!"

"What business?" asked Dooley.

Harriet heaved an exaggerated sigh. "She bought one of those vajayjay steamers and accidentally burned her vajayjay."

"What's a vajayjay?" asked Dooley.

"A woman's business!"

Dooley turned to me. "I don't get it, Max."

I had to admit I didn't get it either. Harriet was now definitely speaking in riddles. Just then, Odelia and Chase walked out of the interview room, while Dexter was led out by a uniformed officer, probably to cool off in one of the cells. "Hey, Harriet—Brutus," said Odelia. "What's up?"

"We found the killer!" Harriet cried.

"Yeah, it's a woman who burned her business on a vajayjay steamer," I said. "Whatever that is."

"Maureen Cranberry," Harriet clarified. "I found her name after a long and very thorough Internet search. She ordered one of Donna's vajayjay steamers and ended up burning her business so she sued Donna for damages and extreme emotional suffering and trauma. She lost, though, but I'm sure she's still very sore."

Odelia smiled. "I'll bet she is."

Chase frowned. "Who are you talking to?"

"She's talking to herself again," Uncle Alec said. "I told you. It's a weird habit she just doesn't seem to be able to shake. Isn't that right, honey?"

"We need to talk to Maureen Cranberry," Odelia said in response. "She might be our killer."

Chase's frown deepened. "Where did that come from, all of a sudden?"

Odelia gave him her best smile. "Just a hunch. Women's intuition. Are you coming?"

"Hey, what about me?" asked Harriet. "I found Maureen!"

"Well, come on, then," Odelia said. "What are you waiting for?"

Four cats tripped after Odelia, drawing puzzled glances from Chase. Then Dooley asked, "What's a vajayjay?"

CHAPTER 19

"So what's with this habit of talking to yourself?" Chase asked. "A habit, I can't help but notice, which seems to grow worse when your cats are around. A lot worse, actually."

Chase was driving his police pickup, Odelia riding shotgun, her assortment of cats in the bed of the truck. Odelia had wanted to put the cats in the backseat, a place usually reserved for arrestees, but Chase had vocally demurred. Claimed he'd just cleaned up the vomit from the last drunk and disorderly he'd arrested and didn't want to have to scrape a bunch of hairballs from the backseat now that he got it all nice and puke-free again.

Odelia shrugged. "It's just a bad habit, Chase. Get over it."

"No, but why does it grow worse when your cats are around? It's almost as if you're talking to them, and they're talking back to you."

She let rip a careless laugh. "Talking to my cats—you should hear yourself, Detective Kingsley. How crazy that sounds."

He smiled. "I know it sounds crazy, but please bear with

me. Isn't it possible that those amazing powers of intuition you always claim to possess—"

"I don't *claim* to possess amazing powers of intuition. I *have* amazing powers of intuition."

"Okay, I'll grant you that. But isn't it possible that those amazing powers of intuition are somehow connected to that ragtag collection of felines you surround yourself with?" He held up his hand. "I know this sounds crazy, but I've given it a lot of thought."

"Have you now? That must have been quite the effort."

He gave her a comical look. "It's been scientifically proven that humans and their pets share a sacred bond of some kind. That they somehow influence each other. All I'm saying is that it's possible that having those cats around has a positive influence on your ability to sniff out clues and find out stuff."

"It's possible," she agreed. Little did he know how possible it really was!

He gave her a keen look. "You know what? I think I just discovered your little secret."

She swallowed away an uncomfortable lump. "You have?"

"Sure. Those cats bring out the best in you."

She smiled with relief. "Of course they do."

"So when are you going to tell me how the name Maureen Cranberry came up?"

She thought quick. "I did a long and very thorough Internet search, and discovered that Maureen bought one of those vagina steamers Donna sells on her site. Maureen ended up burning her business and suing Donna for damages and extreme emotional suffering and trauma."

"Don't tell me. She lost?"

"She did."

"Which makes her a great suspect in my book," Chase grunted. "Great work, Odelia. You're quickly becoming my favorite ace sleuth."

She gave him a chipper smile. "Gee, thanks, Detective. That means a lot coming from you." Little did he know that the real ace sleuth was riding in the bed of the truck, along with three other ace sleuths.

They'd arrived at Donna's house and Odelia frowned. "Are you sure this is the right way?"

"Yeah. Turns out Maureen Cranberry is one of Donna's neighbors. And get this. She's a member of the same neighborhood association Alpin Carré belongs to." He gestured to the small monitor in the center of the console, where Mrs. Cranberry's file had been pulled up.

Odelia squinted at the screen. "This is all gibberish, Chase. What am I looking at?"

"She was at the demonstration this morning. The one where Alpin was arrested? Officers took down the names of everyone present and Mrs. Cranberry was one of them."

Chase pulled the car over onto the shoulder and got out. Across the street, a more modest dwelling than Donna Bruce's majestic mansion stood, a lone mailbox announcing here lived Maureen Cranberry.

She also got out and watched as Max, Dooley, Harriet and Brutus crossed the road, making their way past the gate and onto private property. Her very own feline army, she thought with a smile.

Chase rang the bell and soon the gate slid open and they walked up the short paved driveway to the front of the house. Mrs. Cranberry opened the door and watched them arrive, her arms folded across her chest, an expression of suspicion on her face. And as they drew nearer, Odelia saw to her surprise that the woman was the spitting image of Donna Bruce. The same athletic body type, the same facial structure, and the exact same long blond hair. She could have been Donna's sister.

Chase displayed his badge. "Detective Chase Kingsley.

Hampton Cove PD. And this is Odelia Poole. Civilian consultant. We're investigating the murder of one of your neighbors. Donna Bruce."

The woman's scowl deepened. "What's Donna's death got to do with me, Detective?"

"That's what we're here to find out, Mrs. Cranberry. May we come in?"

Reluctantly, the woman stepped aside to allow them inside. To Odelia's surprise, a large picture portrait of Donna Bruce dominated the foyer, and as they passed into the parlor, the covers of every Donna Magazine that had ever been published had been framed and put up on the walls.

"You're quite the fan, aren't you, Mrs. Cranberry?" asked Chase, studying the setup.

"I am," said the woman stiffly. She led the way into the living room, where a life-sized bust of Donna Bruce took center stage. Oddly enough, even the furniture reminded Odelia of Donna, as the exact same furniture had graced her own house.

Maureen Cranberry wasn't merely Donna's double, she'd also copied Donna's interior design, down to the intricate wood floor medallions, depicting the yin and yang symbols, the heavy velvet curtains, and the pink marble walls. Eerie.

Chase, too, seemed taken aback by this extreme case of hero worship, as he was lost for words for a moment. Odelia decided to step into the breach. "Is it true that you sued Donna Bruce a couple of years ago, Mrs. Cranberry?"

Maureen, who'd taken a seat on one of three high back chairs placed in the salon area of the living room, gestured at the other chairs and nodded. "Yes, that's quite true."

Odelia and Chase sat down, the cop taking out his notebook and Odelia asking, "And is it also true that you lost the case?"

"Yes, unfortunately I did."

"But the incident doesn't seem to have turned you off Donna?"

For the first time, the woman displayed a thin-lipped smile. "No, it didn't."

"So why is that?" asked Chase.

Maureen heaved a little sigh. "Once you're a fan, it's hard to shake that faith. Though I must confess I came close when I had my little… incident."

"With the steamer."

"With the steamer," the woman confirmed.

"But you were seen protesting outside Donna's house this morning," said Chase. "That's not the kind of behavior one would expect from a die-hard fan such as yourself."

"I—I must confess I only joined the protest to take a closer look at Donna's house and—and perhaps even catch a glimpse of Donna herself."

Something occurred to Odelia. "How long have you lived here, Mrs. Cranberry?"

The woman smiled. "I moved in about six months after Donna moved in. Yes, I'm a stalker, Miss Poole, though not the dangerous kind, I can assure you."

"And yet you sued Donna when the contraption you bought from her website malfunctioned, you joined the neighborhood protest against the wall she was building, and…" Chase leaned forward in his chair, tapping his notebook smartly. "… perhaps exacted your own kind of revenge when the lawsuit you filed against your idol was thrown out?"

Maureen shook her head decidedly. "I would never do that. I would never harm Donna. Ask anyone. I was her biggest fan and it pained me to have to file charges against her. I tried to get donna.vip to reimburse me and compensate me for the damage their steamer caused but they simply refused. Filing that suit was the only recourse I had to get my money back."

"And you insist losing the lawsuit didn't inspire you to take revenge in some other way?"

"It did not. Like I said, I would never do anything to hurt Donna. She was my role model, and not just mine. A lot of women looked up to her for advice and leadership. She was an amazing person. One of a kind." She sighed deeply. "She will be sorely missed."

Chase sat back. "Where were you this morning at seven, Mrs. Cranberry?"

"I was over at Alpin's house. Alpin Carré? He's the leader of the neighborhood association and was organizing the protest. We were preparing for the demonstration outside Donna's house. We met at six as we still had a lot of ground to cover. Banners to prepare and signs to put together. Some of the other women brought cake and Alpin provided coffee and tea. We made a fun time of it. We finally set out to march on Donna's house at nine." She shook her head. "If only I'd known Donna had passed away, I would never have come."

There was a sound from the next room, and Maureen sat up with a start.

"Is anyone else here?" asked Chase, his hand moving to his holster.

"No. I live all by myself," said Maureen, a trembling hand moving to her lips.

Chase got up and moved over without making a sound, treading carefully. He'd taken out his gun and was aiming it in the direction of the noise. For a moment Odelia wondered if Donna's killer was now coming after Donna lookalikes as well. She followed at a safe distance, Maureen right behind her, her hand on Odelia's shoulder, as they slowly made their way to the next room.

"What's in there?" Odelia whispered.

"The kitchen," Maureen whispered back. Then she added, "I must have left the door open!"

That bit of information, coupled with the grunt of astonishment from Chase, told Odelia who the intruder was even before she'd reached the door and entered the kitchen.

Three cats sat looking up at them from the kitchen floor, with one cat seated on the kitchen counter, snacking on a very delicious-looking meatloaf: Max. When he finally noticed they were no longer alone, Max looked up, his face covered in crumbs of meatloaf. "Oops," he said.

CHAPTER 20

For the rest of the day, I was confined to the house. House arrest, Odelia called it. Bummer. Luckily, Dooley had opted to stay behind and share my punishment. Harriet and Brutus, not surprisingly, had not. They were out and about somewhere, continuing their investigation. Harriet, after having supplied Odelia with the identity of the vajayjay woman, had become cocky, and now truly believed she was the second coming of Sherlock Holmes or something, and no longer needed my or Dooley's assistance in solving this particularly heinous crime.

Good for her. If she didn't need me, I certainly didn't need her. But if she thought she could catch Donna's killer, she was dead wrong. What she hadn't grasped was that Maureen Cranberry was innocent, which meant she'd led Odelia and Chase on a wild goose chase.

At least I'd had some prime meatloaf. Whatever Maureen Cranberry's faults, she prepared one mean meatloaf. The meat had been tender, succulent and tasty. Just the way I like it.

I opened one eye when Dooley's insufferable snuffling

told me he was somewhere nearby. He looked up at me expectantly. The moment Odelia had delivered the verdict, I'd plunked myself down in my usual spot on the couch and hadn't moved from it. I swear, this diet was slowly killing me, not only robbing me of my physical strength but also of my will to live.

"What do you want, Dooley?" I grumbled, closing my one eye again.

"Aren't we going to continue our investigation?" he asked excitedly.

"What investigation? If you hadn't noticed, we're grounded. We're not going anywhere anytime soon."

"But we have the computer! We can find clues, just like Harriet found that clue about the woman with her burnt business."

I groaned. "If you hadn't noticed, Dooley, that was a rubbish clue. Nothing came of it."

"That's because it was Harriet finding that clue," he said cleverly. "But we're not Harriet, Max. We're the real sleuths in this household. If we put our minds to it, I'm sure we'll find out more than Harriet ever could."

I opened my eyes. Had Dooley just delivered an intelligent statement? I believed he had. And it was so unlike Dooley to make sense that I actually sat up and took notice. "What did you just say?"

"That we're better sleuths than Harriet and Brutus?"

I nodded. "You have a point, Dooley. We *are* better sleuths. In fact we're ace sleuths."

Reluctantly, I abandoned my spot and jumped down from the couch. Dooley had already taken up position in front of the computer and I joined him. We both stared at the screen, which was black.

"So… how does this work, exactly?" I asked. I have to confess I'm not much of a computer cat. I love lying down on the keyboard when Odelia is working, and making sure she can't see the screen, but that's as far as my knowledge of computers goes, to be perfectly honest.

"Just do something, Max," Dooley suggested. "If Harriet can do it, so can we."

He was right, and his statement totally galvanized me. So did the fact that my tummy was full of that delicious meat-loaf. Odelia might not like it when I eat my fill, but I certainly did. I took a stab at the keyboard and to my surprise the screen flickered to life.

"Hey! How did you do that?" asked Dooley.

"No idea. I just did this…" I stabbed at the keyboard again and some letters appeared on the screen.

"Oh, my God, Max. You can type!"

"Yes, I can!" I said enthusiastically, and stabbed at the keyboard some more. More letters appeared, forming one long word that didn't make any sense. But it was something. We were going places! I decided to use the backspace key to remove all those funny symbols and start over. So I carefully typed in donna.vip and we landed on Donna's website. There were a lot of funny things for sale there, so for the next half hour or so, Dooley and I had fun clicking through to the pages of all these items and reading the descriptions. There were those jade eggs Gran had ordered, and for the first time we understood they weren't actual eggs but served an entirely different purpose. Something to do with pelvic muscles, whatever that was. And then there was Maureen Cranberry's V-steamer, which appeared to be beneficial for personal hygiene and improved fertility.

"What's fertility, Max?" asked Dooley.

"I think it's a kind of plant."

"Oh, right. Like a fern."

"They must have misspelled ferntility."

"Humans."

136

"Yeah."

There was a lot more stuff, and it was all weird and wonderful, sort of like the Discovery Channel. There was a prisoner's ball and chain, a toothpaste squeezer, nipple clamps, very expensive paper wipes, a pouch with magically charged stones, gold dumbbells for weightlifting, a facial massager, a heated couch, and… the same kind of rocket that Odelia keeps in her bedside drawer but this one was made of gold. It was called a dildo and its purpose wasn't immediately clear to me.

"What does it do, Max?" Dooley asked, staring at the shiny gold object.

"I'm not sure. It says here it's a massager, but I'm not sure what it's supposed to massage."

"It also says it's elegant and decadent, and has to be used with something called lube. What is a lube, Max?"

"Maybe like a long kind of tube?"

We read some more. It was all very confusing.

"What's a G-spot, Max?"

"I have no idea, Dooley." But then I got it. "I think it's one of those spots that are very hard to reach. Like behind the bed or behind the cupboard."

We shared a look of understanding. "So that's why Odelia keeps it in the bedroom."

"In case she needs to reach those hard-to-reach G-spots."

Well, I was sure glad we figured that out. It's not much fun feeling dumb.

I clicked on another link and this time we ended up on a page extolling the virtues of bee sting therapy. "Weird," Dooley said. "Here they say bee stings are actually good for you."

"Well, maybe they are," I said. "Like nettle stings. Remember that one time you stung your nose on those nettles? And Odelia said it was good for you? This is probably the same thing."

"But then why did Donna end up dead?"

"Well, too much of a good thing isn't good at all, I suppose."

"Like when you eat too many Cat Snax?"

"I'm not sure you can eat too many Cat Snax, Dooley. At least I've never had too many."

"That's true," he admitted. "Me neither."

Just then, there was a loud rap on the glass sliding door, which was now closed due to my house arrest. We hopped down from our perch on the computer table and wandered over. To my pleasant surprise, it was Gran. But to my less pleasant surprise, she appeared incapable of opening the sliding door from the outside. She was shouting something, though. It sounded a lot like, "Has the UPS guy brought another one of my packages?!"

I shook my head and shouted back, "No, he hasn't!"

"Darn!" she yelled, and then stalked off.

"Hey! Aren't you going to let us out?!" I yelled, but she was already gone.

Dooley sat chuckling next to me. I turned to him. "What's so funny?"

"I wonder what she ordered this time. Those dumbbells, that toothpaste squeezer, or that dildo."

"I don't think she would order a dildo."

"And why is that?"

"Marge cleans your house, doesn't she? So why would Gran need to reach those hard-to-reach G-spots?"

"You've got a point, Max."

"Of course I have. I'm very clever."

CHAPTER 21

*I*t was dinner time at the Pooles, and as usual Uncle Alec and Chase had been invited. Dad was master of his domain again—in other words, the barbecue set—and before long a wonderful time was had by all. Well, almost all, as Odelia had locked Max up in the house. She couldn't risk him hanging around all that raw meat. He would have a conniption fit if she tried to keep him away from all that juicy temptation. And to show him she didn't have a heart of stone, she'd given him an extra helping of Vena's diet kibble. Not that he seemed to appreciate it. He'd told her there was only so much cardboard one could stomach, and he'd already had his fill and then some.

It was a hard lesson to learn for the big, red cat, but one that was absolutely necessary. If he kept eating like this, he'd simply dig his own grave with his teeth, the poor baby, and she did not want that on her conscience.

Harriet and Brutus had shown up just when the meat was starting to give off its delicious scent, but when she cut a glance to Harriet, the gorgeous Persian had sadly shaken her head. So far she hadn't discovered a thing. Brutus, who'd immediately pounced on some slivers Dad had cut from the steaks, didn't seem to have any news for her either. That only left Dooley, but all he said was that he'd finally discovered how she cleaned those hard-to-reach spots in her bedroom, and given her a big, fat wink. Weird. Then she remembered she'd left the computer running. Oh, dear. She hoped she'd turned on Parental Control. There was so much on the Internet her cats did not need to see.

Uncle Alec walked up to her, a can of Heineken in his hand. "And? Any luck with the Cranberry woman?"

"Nope. Turns out she had an alibi, just like everyone else in this case."

"Dang. She looked promising."

"She did," Odelia agreed. "Very promising. Just like the ex-husband looked promising, the boyfriend looked promising, and the leader of the home owner's association looked promising."

"Tough day, huh?" asked her uncle, shooting her a keen look.

"Yeah, pretty tough," she admitted. "We keep catching breaks that turn out not to be breaks after all."

"What about your cats?" he asked. "They usually provide the telling clue."

"So far my cats have provided me nothing but trouble," she admitted, and told her uncle about Max's embarrassing behavior at Maureen Cranberry's place.

"So that's why my meatball went missing from my meatball sub," said her uncle with a grin.

"It seems he's eating everything he can get his paws on. Ever since I put him on a diet he's been totally insufferable. It has taken his focus completely off trying to find Donna's killer. All he's interested in is finding food, not clues."

"That'll pass," her uncle assured her. "He just needs some adjusting is all. When your aunt put me on a diet the hardest part were those first few days. Once I got past that it was smooth sailing all the way."

She glanced down at her uncle's rotund belly. Pity Aunt Ginny was gone. Alec could have used one of her patent diets right now. But who was going to put him on one? Certainly not her. She had a hard enough time trying to keep Max to his diet, and he was just a cat.

Chase came ambling up, also a can of Heineken in hand. "So? Another long day at the office, huh? Time for some R&R."

"Speak for yourself," grunted Chief Alec. "When dinner is over I'm heading straight back to the station. I've got a ton of paperwork to finish. What about you, Odelia?"

"I have an article to write," she confessed. She'd started writing it when they came back from Maureen Cranberry, but she still had to put the finishing touches on the piece. "The paper is going to print tomorrow and Dan wants the article done."

"On the Donna Bruce case?" asked Chase.

"Yep. I don't really know what to write, as we're nowhere near figuring out what happened, but deadlines are deadlines."

"And what are you up to, Chase?" asked the Chief.

"Well, I was actually thinking about asking out your niece, but I have a feeling she's about to blow me off."

Odelia looked up in surprise. "You wanted to take me out tonight?"

"I promised I was going to, remember? And you told me you were going to think about it."

"I know, but I figured, with this whole Donna Bruce thing..."

He smiled. "There will always be work, Odelia. You can't let it interfere with your personal life."

"He's right," Uncle Alec grunted. "You never know how

much time you're going to have with your loved ones. If I'd known that back when Ginny was still alive, I'd have spent a lot more time with her. Now it's too late." He looked somber for a moment, the memory obviously still haunting him.

Odelia placed a hand on her uncle's arm. "You had a lot of good years together, Uncle Alec. You should be grateful you got to spend them with Aunt Ginny as long as you did."

He gave her a weak smile. "You're right, honey. And I am. Grateful, I mean. I'm just telling you not to make the same mistake I did. Putting work before everything else. This case will get solved, or it won't. You can't let that stop you from spending time with this hotshot detective over here. At least if that's what you want."

Now it was her turn to smile. "What are you saying? I should give this hotshot detective a shot?"

"He's not a bad guy," said Chief Alec. "He's young and impetuous, of course, but then all guys are at his age. But with some patience and effort I think we might make something out of him yet."

Chase gave the chief a playful shove. "Thanks, old-timer. I appreciate the vote of confidence. So what about it, Odelia? Wanna catch a movie with this hotshot detective?"

And she was just about to respond in the affirmative, when a wide-eyed young man dressed in a brown uniform showed up in the backyard, carrying a huge box. Judging from the logo on his uniform he was the UPS guy, and when he was done scanning the small group gathered around the barbecue set, he gulped and asked, "Who is Vesta Muffin? I'm looking for a Vesta Muffin."

Gran seemed reluctant to reveal herself, so finally Mom had to step up and tell the guy, "That's my mother. Why didn't you ring at the front door?"

"I did. More than once. Can I leave this with you, ma'am? It's... buzzing."

He placed the bulky package on the lawn and quickly took a few steps back.

"Buzzing?" asked Mom, eyeing the package with suspicion. Then she turned to Gran. "Mom. What did you order this time?"

"Nothing," said Gran. "Must be some mistake."

"No mistake," said the UPS guy. "You ordered from donna.vip. Paid extra for special delivery. Though nobody told me the package would be alive."

His eyes were wide as he offered Mom the gadget to sign. Mom jotted down her scrawl and the UPS guy immediately was off like a rocket. "Thanks!" he yelled and disappeared from view.

They all gathered around the package, and Odelia discovered that the UPS guy had been right: the thing was buzzing.

"What did you order, Gran?" she asked.

"Nothing!" Gran insisted. "You told me to stop ordering stuff so I did."

Dad bent down, a glass of red wine in his hand, and read from the label on the package. "It says your name right here, Vesta."

"Must be a namesake. Lots of Vestas around."

"Vesta Muffin? Living at this address?"

"Sure. UPS screwed up again. Figures."

She seemed awfully nervous about a simple mistake, though, which told Odelia it wasn't a mistake at all. The only reason she was mad at the UPS guy was that he'd shown up now, when everyone was there, and not a couple of hours earlier, when she could have intercepted the package.

"Well, I guess we better see what's inside," said Uncle Alec, and started removing the packaging. And that's when something came buzzing from inside the box and attached itself to his nose. He swatted it away, and Odelia got a good look at the culprit. It was a bee!

"Gran," she demanded. "Tell me you didn't order a bunch of bees!"

"Of course not!" Gran said. "I'm not crazy. Who orders a bunch of bees?! Not me!"

They all worked together to remove the wrapping, and found themselves staring down at an actual beehive! And its inhabitants were obviously not very happy at having been cooped up for so long, for more than a few of them started flying through the cracks in the cage and zooming around.

"Christ!" Uncle Alec yelled. "Who in their right mind ships a bunch of bees with UPS?!"

"Vesta," said Dad phlegmatically, swatting away a couple of bees buzzing around his wine.

"I think we better call the fire department," Chase said. "Before they all escape and attack us."

"No!" Gran yelled. "You know how much these little suckers cost me?!"

"So you did order them!" Mom yelled, ducking a few particularly pesky bees.

"Of course I did! I need bee therapy! It's going to completely rejuvenate me! I'm going to look decades younger!"

"You're crazy!" Uncle Alec screamed, now running around the yard, chased by a horde of bees.

"Let them sting your butt!" Gran yelled. "It'll clear that cellulite of yours right up!"

And then, as if the bees had gotten the message, the cage completely collapsed, and the entire swarm zoomed up into the air, then swept down upon the Pooles.

"Nice, Mom!" Uncle Alec yelled. "I've been stung!"

"That's great! You needed it!"

Odelia wasn't sure if she needed it or not, but she was pretty sure she didn't want it, so when a dozen bees attacked her, happy to have found a target, she screamed and ducked for cover. It took another half hour for the fire department to arrive, and make short shrift of Gran's bee menace. Gran wasn't happy that her investment was being rounded up and taken away by the burly men in red, but the rest of the family definitely was. By the time the last bee had been taken into custody, it was late.

"So much for our date," Odelia told Chase as she watched the firemen inspect the hive.

"I'll take a rain check," said Chase, scratching at a particularly nasty-looking bee sting.

"I'm sorry about this, Chase. My family is crazy."

"That's okay," he said with a grin. "I'm not all that compos myself."

He placed an arm around her shoulder and she leaned her head against his chest. Between the murder they had to solve and Max's diet shenanigans and her grandmother's Donna obsession, she was glad at least one person in her universe still had his feet on solid ground. And as she watched a red-faced Dad furiously cut up his credit cards, Gran looking on sadly, she had to laugh.

"That's the spirit," Chase murmured. "When you can't beat the crazies, join them." And he placed a tender kiss on her lips.

"Ouch," she said, pulling back. "Bee sting." Right on her bottom lip of all places. Gah.

"Didn't you hear your grandmother? Your lip will look decades younger in the morning."

"Oh, to hell with it," she muttered, and kissed him right back.

CHAPTER 22

*T*hat night, I simply couldn't hold it anymore. If I ate one more chunk of that diet crap I was going to scream. My stomach was grumbling and I was so hungry I thought I was going to die. The worst thing was that Odelia had put me on the scale that evening after she came home from dinner and I'd actually gained weight! How was that even possible?!

Of course she had her explanation ready. According to her it was because of that meatball I'd scarfed down, and that meatloaf I'd polished off at Mrs. Cranberry's house. But I called bullshit on both accounts. How could a little bit of meat result in me gaining weight while I'd been starving all the rest of the day?

I roamed around the house, feeling restless and annoyed, and that's when I discovered that Odelia had left the kitchen window open! So I climbed up onto the sink, careful not to put my paw in the garbage disposal unit, pushed the window open wider, and gracefully hopped down onto the sill and then to the plastic container right underneath it. Odelia uses it to collect the garbage bags and it's the perfect landing place for a big-boned cat like me. I know people are always saying how a cat always lands on its feet. Well, if you're genetically predisposed to be on the more voluminous side, like me, it can be hard to accomplish that feat, especially when jumping down from higher surfaces.

I landed on the container with a heavy thump, and waited for a moment, making sure I hadn't woken up Odelia. Then I jumped down to the patio and padded off, hoping Dooley still had some tasty morsels he wouldn't mind sharing with his best friend.

Unfortunately, when I finally had slipped into the house next door, all the bowls were empty: Dooley's bowl, Harriet's bowl, and even Brutus's bowl! How was that even possible?

I quickly made my way up the stairs, careful not to wake up anyone, and nudged open the door to Marge and Doctor Tex's room. Sure enough, Brutus was asleep on Tex's side of the bed and Harriet on Marge's side. So I tiptoed into Gran's bedroom, which was right down the hall, and found Dooley asleep at the foot of Gran's bed.

"Psssst!" I said, giving Dooley a slight nudge.

"Hrrrmmbl…" he said in response, and just kept on sleeping.

"Dooley! Wake up!"

The beige cat opened one eye and then closed it again. "Hmmmmmmm."

So I hopped up onto the bed—conveniently a lot lower than Odelia's—and kicked him off. I watched in wonder to see if he would magically right himself in midair and hit the floor on all fours. Unfortunately for Dooley he hit the floor with his head instead. It made a nice thunking sound as it did. Hollow. Just as I'd expected.

"What's going on?" Dooley asked as he rubbed the point of impact.

"I'm going foraging," I told him. "And I need my wingcat."

He stared at me. "I can't, Max. My head hurts for some reason."

"Your head is fine. Let's go."

He rubbed the spot for a few beats more, obviously wondering what had happened, then decided to follow me out. "I was dreaming of Harriet," he said. "She told me to use my dildo to reach her G-spot so I did, but then Brutus showed up and burned me with his V-steamer."

"You shouldn't read that kind of stuff before bed, Dooley. You should do like me and dream of steaks and prime ribs and sausages and meatballs and beef tenderloin and..." Well, you get the picture.

We left the house and set out for the great outdoors. I had no idea where we were going but I knew it had to be someplace where we would find food. Lots of food. Any food.

"Where are we going, Max?" asked Dooley after a while.

"Where they have food," I told him.

"And where is that?"

I thought hard, which was difficult as I was so hungry my mental capacity had become impaired. Honestly, how Odelia expected me to catch killers on an empty stomach was beyond me. And then I got it. "Why don't we go check out Donna Bruce's place?"

"Do you think they'll have food there?"

"Well, they have those two mutts. And where there are mutts, there is always food."

That's one of those immutable facts of life, and one you would do well to remember. I know I do. Even at my most feeble, like now, when my survival instincts were kicking in, I still remembered that humans love dogs—even more than they love cats—and always make sure they're well fed. What most humans don't know is that cats can also eat dog food, especially when they're on the verge of dying of starvation, like I was now.

"I don't know, Max," said Dooley. "Those dogs weren't very nice to us the last time."

"They'll be fast asleep by now," I promised him. "We'll just sneak in and out. They won't even know we were there."

Dooley sighed. "Good thing you're my best friend, Max. I would never do this for Brutus."

"Do what?"

"Risk life and limb to get you some dog biscuits."

I gave him a warm smile. "I know, Dooley. And I'm glad you're my friend."

"I would do it for Harriet," he continued musingly. "But only if she asked me. Once upon a time I would have done it without asking, but those days are definitely over."

"Wow. Love doesn't live there anymore, huh?"

"Where?" he asked, puzzled.

"It's an expression. It means you've stopped loving Harriet."

"I never loved Harriet," he said annoyedly. "I liked Harriet a lot. There's a difference."

"Of course there is."

We were trotting along the main road, cars passing us by, making great time, and I was actually starting to perk up a little. The prospect of digging into Rex and Rollo's bowls and fishing out the best bits almost made me feel giddy. A woman like Donna, rich beyond compare, probably spent a fortune on dog food, reserving only the best and most expensive stuff for her beloved mutts. I just hoped they hadn't eaten all of it.

"Do you think Harriet will ever break up with Brutus?" asked Dooley.

"Why? I thought you only 'liked' her?"

"I do. That's why I feel it's my duty to look out for her. And I don't think Brutus is right for her, Max. I really don't."

"I think he is. Those two deserve each other," I said. And

if I sounded bitter that's because I was. Harriet was trying to steal my thunder. Presenting herself as the prime sleuth in the Poole household. Well, I wasn't having it. There was only one prime sleuth and that was me. At least when I was properly fed and my brain was working at full capacity.

"Brutus has changed," Dooley admitted, still harping on the same theme. "He's become more sedate. Less of a bully."

"I told you. He's henpecked now. Domesticated. He won't give us any more trouble."

"Do you really believe that, Max?"

"Yes, I do." No, I didn't. Bullies like Brutus never really change. Though we had reached some kind of understanding lately. A détente, like the US and the USSR had in Cold War days.

"Tell me something, Max."

I grunted, hoping he'd finally change the subject. All this talk of Harriet and Brutus was getting on my nerves. "What?"

"When Harriet kissed you, what did it feel like?"

"Wet."

"Did you feel butterflies fluttering around in your tummy? A choir of angels singing in the sky? The scent of blossoms filling your nostrils? A feeling that all was well with the world?"

"I felt an urge to slap her, if that's what you mean."

He gave me a dark scowl. Obviously that wasn't the answer he'd been looking for.

Lucky for me we'd finally reached the Donna Bruce place. All was dark, which was a good sign. I just hoped Rex and Rollo would prove as dumb as they looked and wouldn't chase two innocent cats trying to steal their food after hours. We approached with stealth and bated breath, and walked around the back, just like that morning. The pool area was deserted, and there was no sign of the two hyped-up poodles.

"Looks promising," I whispered.

"Why are you whispering?" Dooley whispered back.

Some questions are just too dumb to dignify with a response so I didn't respond. Instead, I padded up to the back door but found it locked. Obviously. And thus the tedious task of finding an access point began. I finally found a ground floor window that was ajar and attempted to get in that way. Unfortunately, because of my big bones, I didn't fit. So I told Dooley to give it a try. It was a tight fit but he managed. Once he was inside, he whispered, "What do I do now?"

"Now you go in search of food and bring it to me," I instructed my feeble-minded friend.

He gave me two claws up and disappeared from sight. I waited patiently for his return, all the while trying to ignore my rumbling stomach. I'd never known hunger before, and now I understood what all the hungry animals in the world must experience on a daily basis. It wasn't a lot of fun.

And I'd just wandered off in the direction of the pool, when I caught movement inside the house. I walked up to the glass doors and peeked inside. One of the many advantages us felines have over humans is that we can see in the dark. And what I saw in the dark was… Donna Bruce!

I staggered back in shock and horror. What the… After gathering my courage, I approached the window once more. And sure enough, Donna Bruce was walking around inside, dressed in a white nightgown, carrying some kind of smoking contraption in her hands and flitting to and fro as she waved the smoky thing along the walls, moved it past the furniture, and generally seemed to be performing some kind of strange ritual.

I'd never seen a dead person walking around before, so I had my face glued to the glass all the while. Now that I was over my first reaction of fear, the phenomenon was kinda fascinating. So this was what a ghost looked like, huh? Cool!

Then she disappeared from sight and the show was over.

Lost in thought, I moved back to where I'd left a Dooley eager to find food for me. What I found was a Dooley scared stiff.

"I saw a ghost!" he cried.

"Me too. Where's my food?"

"I saw the ghost of Donna Bruce!"

"I know. So where's my food?"

"She's dead and she's still walking around!"

"My food, Dooley!"

He stared at me, not comprehending. Then he got it. "Oh, there is no food. I think they moved the dogs. There's no sign of Rex and Rollo. But I saw the ghost of Donna Bruce!"

Crap. I didn't know much about ghosts, but what I did know was that they didn't eat. So we'd come all this way for nothing? Crappity crap! But then it dawned on me. If I told Odelia we'd seen the ghost of Donna Bruce she might be so happy she gave me some Cat Snax!

And as Dooley and I began the long trek back to home and hearth, that thought was the only thing that kept me going. That and the notion that we'd finally bested Harriet at the sleuthing thing. Cause if that really was Donna's ghost, she'd be able to tell us who killed her, wouldn't she? Of course she would. Case closed! Cat Snax here I come!

CHAPTER 23

*O*delia woke up from the scuffle of paws and the clicking of claws against the side of the bed. There were hushed voices and she knew what was going on. Max was trying to jump up on the bed, proving he wasn't too fat, and Dooley was giving him a boost but failing to apply sufficient thrust to propel the overweight cat up and away.

She rolled over and tried to go back to sleep. It was still dark out and she so did not want to get up. After the bee incident there had been a lot of shouting and recriminations being hurled about, and it had taken forever to calm down all parties and clear the house and garden of the last straggling bees. Now all she wanted to do was sleep.

"Pssst! Odelia!"

"Just lemme sleeeeep," she murmured.

"Push harder, Dooley!"

"I'm pushing as hard as I can, Max!"

"Odelia! We've got news for you!"

"Tell me in the morning."

"This can't wait! We saw a ghost!"

"Max, I'm getting squished here."

"That's not possible. You're just not pushing hard enough."

"You're too heavy!"

"No, I'm not. You're just being lazy is all."

There was the sound of a heavy object dropping to the floor and Dooley squealing in pain. Odelia sat up with a jerk. "Will you two cut it out already? I'm trying to get some sleep here."

"Max sat on me!"

"I did not! You dropped me!"

With a loud groan of exasperation she switched on the light and peered over the edge of the bed. Max was sitting on top of Dooley's face and Dooley did not seem happy about it.

"Max. Get off Dooley. Dooley, you should know better than to try and lift Max."

"I know," Dooley said once Max had shifted his butt. "But he insists it's what friends do."

"If you were really my friend you'd simply do as I tell you and give me a boost," Max grumbled.

"What's all this about a ghost?" Odelia muttered, supporting her head on her hand, her eyes drooping closed again.

"We saw the ghost of Donna Bruce. She was haunting her own house. Can I get a snack now?" asked Max.

Odelia's eyes flashed open. "What were you two doing at Donna's house?"

"We were… investigating," Max said.

"And also looking for food," Dooley added, earning him a scowl from Max.

"And then you saw Donna's ghost," Odelia said skeptically.

"Yes, we did," Dooley said. "I saw her first, as I was inside the house looking for Rex and Rollo's bowls. Max was waiting outside cause he couldn't fit through the window."

"Too much information, Dooley," Max hissed.

"No, that's fine," said Odelia. She knew Dooley would never lie to her, which meant they really had seen something. She very much doubted it would be a ghost, since ghosts didn't exist, but there must have been someone lurking about. "What did she look like, this ghost?"

"She looked exactly like Donna," said Dooley.

"Spitting image," Max agreed.

"And what does Donna look like?"

Dooley thought for a moment. "Well, she's a woman, for one thing."

"Long hair. Long white dress," Max added.

"She was sort of floating around. Barefoot."

"And she was carrying some kind of smoky thing, doing some kind of ritual."

"Oh, that's right," said Dooley enthusiastically. "There was an awful lot of smoke."

Odelia frowned. What little she knew about ghosts was that they wore whatever they died in, and since Donna had died in the nude, with only a towel to protect her modesty, this ghostly apparition most probably was not Donna. Still, it was obvious Max and Dooley had seen someone poking around Donna's house in the middle of the night, so…

She picked up her phone from the nightstand and dialed Chase's number. After a few rings a groggy voice muttered, "'lo?"

"Hey, Chase. Odelia. We have to check out Donna's place. Someone's prowling around."

There was a momentary silence, then, "You're at Donna's house?"

"No, I'm in bed right now."

"So… how do you know there's a prowler on the loose?"

"Women's—"

"Intuition. I get the drill. Meet me at the house. I'll be there in five."

She bit her lip. She should probably have thought this through a little more. Now Chase would think she was psychic. Unless there was no one out there, in which case he'd think she was nuts.

"Can we come?" asked Max.

"No, you can't," she said. "You're still grounded, mister."

"But we found the ghost!"

"You shouldn't have been out there!"

"But… we're just trying to help. Find the killer and all that."

She shot him a look of censure. He was right, of course. They had found a valuable clue. "All right. You can come. But on one condition."

"Anything!"

"From now on you're going to stick to your diet. No more sneaking off in search of food. Is that understood?"

Max wavered. This was obviously a hard decision to make. Finally his curiosity to find out more about this ghost won out and he nodded. "Oh, all right. I'll stick to my diet from now on."

"Good." She got dressed in jeans and a hooded sweatshirt, slipped her feet into a pair of sneakers and snatched her smartphone from the nightstand.

"Don't forget to take your dildo," said Dooley helpfully.

Her hand paused. "What did you just say?"

"Your dildo," Dooley said. "To reach those hard-to-reach G-spots. Who knows where this ghost is hiding, right?"

She frowned down at Dooley and Max, both looking up at her with expressions of such innocence and guilelessness she couldn't help but smile. "Of course I'll take my dildo. I never leave home without it." She snapped the plastic object from the drawer and put it in her pocket. And as she walked down the stairs she swore never to let those cats near the Internet again. Ever.

CHAPTER 24

*S*he arrived at the house just as Chase rolled up in his pickup truck and parked right behind hers. He got out, his hair tousled and dressed in sturdy jeans, check flannel shirt and cowboy boots. "So what's this about a prowler? And don't give me that women's intuition line again."

"I got a call just now from one of Donna's neighbors walking his dog. He said he saw someone move around inside the house."

"Who called?"

"I'm sorry but I can't tell you. A reporter has to protect her sources."

He gave her an intense look. "Haven't we moved beyond that crap, Odelia?"

She lifted her shoulders in a shrug and turned toward the house. "What can I say? My sources trust me to protect their confidentiality and anonymity and I owe it to them to respect that."

"Of course you do," he grumbled as he fell into step beside

her. He looked down when he saw movement and started. "You brought your cats along?"

"Always."

He shook his head. "You are one special cookie, Odelia."

She hooked her arm through his. "But you like special cookies, right?"

He eyed her warmly. "You know I do. Now let's catch ourselves a prowler, shall we?"

They arrived at the house and Odelia watched her cats sneak around the back. A sliver of fear suddenly settled around her heart. "So how do you want to do this?"

"Very carefully," Chase said, and peered into one of the windows on the ground floor. "I don't see a thing."

"Maybe they're upstairs." Or maybe they left already. Or maybe her cats were delusional.

Chase moved to the front door and studied the lock for a moment. Then he took a small pouch from his pocket and extracted a metal tool that she seemed to recognize from her frequent visits to the dentist. Chase inserted it into the lock, then added a second metal tool and messed around with them for a while. The door suddenly clicked open and they were in.

"I didn't know you burgled houses for a living!" she whispered as they stepped inside.

"Back when I was employed by the NYPD I had a buddy who was a converted crook. He taught me a few tricks of his trade. You never know when this kind of stuff comes in handy. Like now."

"Can you teach me?"

He grinned. "If you teach me about women's intuition."

"I can't. It's called women's intuition for a reason."

"So it's like some kind of secret only shared by women, huh?"

"Something like that."

They both took out their smartphones to light their way, and quickly inspected the ground floor but found it to be completely deserted. Odelia sniffed the air, and thought the house smelled an awful lot of pot, for some reason. She noticed Max gesturing at her through a half-opened window so she opened the window further and let him in. "Remember what I told you," she said. "No looking for food. Only clues."

"Clues, yes. Food, no. Gotcha."

She followed Chase up the stairs, going from room to room. With two bathrooms and six bedrooms, the place was pretty expansive, and they'd finally reached the master bedroom when both their beams of light fell on a lone figure asleep in the bed. They halted in their tracks.

"What the..." Chase muttered. He held up a hand, balling it into a fist in some kind of Special Forces command, and proceeded further into the room, Odelia hanging back. She saw that he'd drawn his gun and was pointing it at the intruder. She just hoped it wasn't Donna's ghost because she didn't think ghosts responded well to gunfire.

Chase had reached the bed and was staring down at the sleeping figure, a frown creasing his brow.

"Who is it?" she asked from the door.

He beckoned her over, holstering his service weapon. And as she joined him, she saw the figure was a woman, dressed in a long, flowing white robe, barefoot and with long dark hair. And it definitely wasn't Donna Bruce.

"She looks familiar somehow," said Chase. "Like I've seen her before somewhere."

And then it dawned on her. "But that's Zelda Yoke. The actress. She starred in those *Star Cars* movies. Remember? Where a bunch of cars turn out to be these big robot warriors, fighting other big robot warriors in space. She made a bunch of those."

"I remember. Weren't she and Donna Bruce locked in some kind of rivalry?"

"They were. Donna starred in the more popular *Star Rigs* franchise, where a bunch of trucks turn out to be big robot warriors, fighting other big robot warriors in space."

As the leading ladies of the two nearly identical franchises, the two stars fought a bitter battle for years. Finally, Donna retired from the franchise and acting to focus on her website, and Zelda's star had faded away when the fifth and final movie in the *Star Cars* series bombed at the box office.

Chase shook the woman's shoulder and she stirred, smacking her lips. "Donna? Is that you?" she murmured. When she opened her eyes and saw two strangers staring down at her, she yelped in sudden fear. "Who the hell are you?"

"Hampton Cove Police, ma'am. May I ask what you're doing in Donna Bruce's bed?"

The woman blinked. "Why, Donna invited me, of course. I'm her starring guest."

"You are aware that Mrs. Bruce passed away this morning, ma'am?"

"Of course I'm aware Donna passed away. Why do you think I'm here?"

"You mean she invited you before she died?"

"No, she invited me after she died. Told me to come to her home and get in touch with her spirit." She sat up, a glazed look in her eyes. "Donna and I have always had a very strong connection. Sisters from another mister is what we were. Kindred spirits. So when she died I felt a very powerful disturbance in the force and I just knew I had to come here."

"I'm afraid you're trespassing, ma'am."

"But Donna wants me here. She needs me here. I'm telling you her spirit reached out to me."

"Why don't you get dressed and come with me?"

"Come with you?" She frowned. "Who are you again?"

"Hampton Cove Police. And I'm afraid you're under arrest for trespassing."

"But I can't be. I keep telling you but you won't listen. Donna invited me. I'm a guest."

"Were you burning something downstairs, Mrs. Yoke?" asked Odelia, remembering Dooley's words.

The former actress smiled. "You're very perceptive. I was burning incense. To ward off the bad spirits and to summon Donna's spirit."

"And did it work?" asked Chase.

"Not yet. But I'm sure she'll be here any moment now." The woman glanced around, as if fully expecting Donna to suddenly materialize out of thin air. "She invited me here, you know."

"Of course she did," said Chase. "Now come along, Mrs. Yoke."

"Are you familiar with my work, Officer?"

"As a matter of fact I am," said Chase as he escorted the woman from the room.

"And what was your favorite? I liked the first *Star Cars* the most. That one was a huge hit."

"Yes, it was," said Chase, and helped the actress down the stairs. It was a little sad to see her like this, Odelia thought. She had been wonderful in those *Star Cars* movies.

"Did you know I do all my own stunts?"

"Is that a fact?"

"Donna never did. Everything you see in those *Star Rigs* movies is all CGI. With *Star Cars* what you see is what you get. It's all real. All me."

"If you don't mind my asking, where were you this morning around seven, Mrs. Yoke?"

"This morning around seven?" They'd reached the foyer and Chase opened the front door to escort the woman out.

"Why, I was reaching out to Donna, of course. We're connected on a higher level, you know. Soul sisters."

"Mind the step."

And as the woman padded barefoot along the drive in the direction of Chase's pickup, Odelia and Chase at her elbows making sure she didn't trip and fall, Odelia thought they'd just closed this case. It was now obvious to her that the intense rivalry that had existed between the two actresses all these years had finally driven Zelda Yoke crazy, inducing her to commit this atrocious act of violence and get rid of her 'soul sister' once and for all.

The cats came tripping behind her. They, too, seemed pleased as punch at this unexpected development. Mostly because they'd beaten Harriet at her own game, and possibly because Max had found something to eat after all, judging from the crumbs of dog biscuit covering his lips.

She decided he'd earned it. And as Chase placed Zelda in the back of his car and locked the door, he said, "I think the combination of your intuition and your secretive informant may just have cracked this case, Odelia."

"I think so, too," she said, directing a commiserating glance at Zelda, who sat muttering to herself, rocking back and forth. "What a sad ending, though, right?"

"Yeah, I loved those *Star Cars* movies. They were da bomb."

"Da bomb?" she laughed. "The nineties called, they want their bomb back."

"Laugh all you want. *Star Cars* was great fun."

"I was more into *Star Rigs*."

"*Star Rigs* was clearly a rip-off of *Star Cars*."

"I'm pretty sure *Star Rigs* came first."

"And I'm pretty sure you're wrong."

"Don't tell me you're a Zelda Yoke fan."

"Don't tell me you're a Donna Bruce fan."

Odelia held her hand up in the *Star Rigs* salute, which was a fist with her pinkie finger sticking out. "*Star Rigs* forever, buddy."

Chase made the *Star Cars* salute, a fist with his thumb sticking out sideways. "*Star Cars* all the way, babe."

And the age-old rivalry would have caused two more casualties if Zelda hadn't at that moment rolled down her window and asked, "Can we go now? Donna is waiting for me."

"Waiting for you where?" asked Chase.

The actress raised her eyes to the sky. "Why, amongst the stars, of course."

"Of course," said Chase with a grin at Odelia, and got into the car.

Odelia watched him drive off. "Well, you guys did good."

"Do you think she did it?" asked Dooley.

"I'm pretty sure she did."

"Yay!" Max said, pumping the air with his paw. "So can I have some Cat Snax now?"

She smiled. "Yes, you can. But then you're going back on the diet, all right?"

"Yes!" Max exclaimed, exchanging a high five with Dooley. "We did it, Dooley!"

"Case closed?"

"Case closed," Odelia agreed.

CHAPTER 25

I was lounging on the windowsill, the sun streaming in through the window, having a well-deserved nap. I'd solved the case. I'd enjoyed my Cat Snax. Now all I had to do was rub Harriet's face in my victory and my triumph was complete.

Dooley was lying next to me, also in deep slumber, while Odelia had left to interview Zelda Yoke, the actress who'd murdered her long-time rival. According to Odelia it was a sad case, though I didn't see it that way. Rivalry amongst actors has always existed. Bette Davis and Joan Crawford. Olivia de Havilland and Joan Fontaine. Tom and Jerry. The list goes on and on. Only this time a line had been crossed and one rival had actually murdered another rival. I guess it's just one of those things. I think they call it an occupational hazard. I'm sure you can even take out insurance against it.

"Max, you devil," suddenly a voice rang out nearby.

I opened one eye and saw that Harriet had drifted into the room.

"Hey, Harriet. How's things?"

"Things are lousy. You just solved my case without me! You actually went around my back and solved my case!"

"Hey, I just had one of my famous hunches. You can't blame me for being brilliant."

She seemed really fired up, for she was pacing the room, her face all scrunched up in an expression of extreme upset. "This was my case, Max. My case. I was going to solve it."

"By surfing the web. Riiiight," I said, my voice dripping with sarcasm.

"It's the new way! The modern way."

"Solving a murder case without leaving the house? That's just ridiculous!"

"No, it's not. Hercule Poirot solved murder cases just by letting his little gray cells do all the work. And he didn't even have a computer!"

"He had that gumshoe, that Hastings guy to do all the legwork for him," I reminded her. Which actually wasn't such a bad idea. Maybe next case I could get Dooley to do all the walking around—which is kinda exhausting, you have to admit, not to mention tedious—and then I'd simply put two and two together and come up with a brilliant solution. Just like that pint-sized Belgian detective!

Brutus had also joined us and was sticking his nose in the air and sniffing. "Cat Snax?" he asked.

"Yup. My reward for cracking another case."

He grimaced. "Good for you, Max. Though I wouldn't advertise the fact too much. Harriet's been sore as a gumboil ever since she found out."

Harriet, who'd disappeared into the kitchen, now returned, and Brutus was right. She was sore as a gumboil. Maybe even sorer. Like two gumboils. "I can't believe Odelia let you skip your diet!" she cried. "Cat Snax? Really? You should be ashamed of yourself!"

I wasn't following. "Ashamed of myself for cracking this case?"

"No, for manipulating Odelia into letting you cheat on your diet."

"It's my reward. I did the work and now I deserve a reward."

"Don't you see that you're endangering yourself with this morbid obesity you're pushing for, Max?"

"Hey, who are you calling morbidly obese?"

"You, Max. You are morbidly obese."

"And you are jealous I cracked the case and you didn't."

"You only think about yourself, don't you? Huh?"

"Who else is there to think about?" I asked, puzzled.

"He's got a point, toots," said Brutus.

She turned on him in a flash. "Oh, now you're taking his side?"

"No, but…"

"You men! You're all the same! Never a thought about anyone but yourselves! Have you ever considered Odelia's feelings, Max?"

"Um…"

"How devastated she's going to be when you die?"

"Well, I don't intend to die anytime soon, so the point is moot."

Dooley, who'd followed the back-and-forth with mild interest, laughed. "Moot. Funny word."

"The way you're going, you are going to die soon, Max. And Odelia is going to be crushed. For some reason—Lord only knows why—she seems to care about you, and the loss will be a blow."

I thought about this. Maybe Harriet was right. If I died—which was a very big if, mind you—Odelia wouldn't take the news well. She did like me a lot. And what was not to like?

I'm funny, charming, handsome, clever and I provide great entertainment.

"Look, I'm not going to die, Harriet," I said. "So you can stop with all the scaremongering. I know you're jealous because I cracked another case and you'll say just about anything to upset me but it's not going to work."

"Good one, bro," Brutus muttered.

I glanced over. Weird. Brutus was taking my side now? This was something new.

"Well, I'll have you know that if you keep digging your grave with your teeth the way you've been doing for some time now you'll be dead within a year. Probably even less. So there."

"Is she right, Max?" asked Dooley. "Are you going to die soon?"

"Of course I'm not going to die! I'm far too young to die!"

"Not if you keep eating those Cat Snax," said Harriet. "That stuff will kill you."

"Pretty tasty, though," Brutus muttered, refusing to meet Harriet's gaze.

"And the same goes for you, Brutus," said Harriet. "If you can't stick to your diet we're finished. Kaput. The end."

He directed a pleading look at her. "Come on, babe. I'm not as fat as Max. Just look at us. He's a lot fatter than me. He's at least twice my size."

"That's because he's a different body type," she snapped.

Brutus lifted his face to me, the look of a long-suffering cat in his eyes. 'See what I'm dealing with here?' the look seemed to say. 'You're not the only cat who's in pain.'

And then I got it. For some reason, Harriet had put her beau on a diet. And knowing Brutus as a great trenchercat, one whose jaws never seemed to stop mauling some little morsel or snack, he was probably in his own private hell right now. And since misery loves company, he was obviously looking upon me as a friend. A fellow sufferer of this diet craze.

"Brutus," Harriet said as she headed for the door. "Are you coming?"

Brutus directed a longing look at the kitchen, where my bowl of Cat Snax stood.

"Brutus! I'm not going to tell you twice!"

The former bully hung his head and shuffled out the door, his proud spirit broken.

"You know? I'm actually feeling sorry for the guy," said Dooley, watching him leave.

"Me too. Who would have thought Harriet could turn into the cat from hell?"

"I did," Dooley said ruefully. "She once accused me of being a spineless yellow-belly."

"But why?"

"For not standing up to you more."

"To me!"

He nodded. "She figured you treated me more like a slave than a friend sometimes, and told me to rise up and not take any more of your crap."

"Why, the little minx! Trying to drive a wedge through our friendship!"

"You have been kind of insufferable lately, though, Max. So maybe Harriet had a point."

"Insufferable? Me? Are you crazy?!"

Dooley winced. "I think it's the diet. It makes you cranky."

"I'm never cranky! I'm the picture of equanimity and poise!"

"I don't know what that means, but you have to admit you have a pretty short fuse these days. I love you, Max, but it's tough being your friend when you're hungry."

I thought about this. Maybe Dooley was right. I did get pretty cranky when I was hungry, and I did have a tendency to take it out on others. I gave him a rueful look. "I'm sorry, buddy. I guess you're right. I don't like feeling hungry, but I shouldn't take it out on you."

"That's all right. I don't like being hungry either. I guess none of us do."

I plunked my head down on my paws. "I know one thing, Dooley."

"What's that?"

"Dieting sucks."

"Well, at least the case is solved. I'm sure Odelia will lighten up now."

"Yeah, at least there's that."

From beyond our garden, Harriet's high-pitched voice reached our ears.

"Brutus! I told you not to eat that mouse!"

"But I like mice!" Brutus said plaintively. "They're full of proteins."

"Too many saturated fats! Now come along. Time for our power walk. Work off that fat!"

I shared a look with Dooley, and we both shook our heads. "Poor Brutus," I said.

CHAPTER 26

"I can't believe she's dead," Zelda wailed. The effect of whatever she'd been on had worn off by now, and she finally seemed to realize what she'd done.

Chase and Odelia were sitting across the table from the actress, whose hands were shackled down. Odelia directed a pleading look at Chase, who took the keys to her cuffs out of his pocket and released the woman.

"She was my best friend!" Zelda continued to wail, gratefully accepting the box of tissues Odelia placed in front of her.

"I thought she was your greatest rival," said Chase.

"She was—but being the greatest rivals created a bond. After my career tanked, Donna was the only one who cared to look me up. She helped me find an apartment when my money ran out and even paid the rent. She was the only true friend I ever had."

Now this was news. "So where do you live now?" asked Odelia.

"Long Island City. I moved out here when Donna moved out here."

"And Donna was paying your rent?"

"She was. Now that she's gone I guess that'll be over."

"Maybe not. Maybe she put a provision in her will for you."

Zelda looked up hopefully. "You think?"

"Didn't you ever talk about this kind of stuff?"

She shook her head. "Donna figured we'd live forever. She refused to discuss death. Said if we just ignored it we might be able to cheat it." She laughed through her tears. "She was a real hoot once you got to know her."

"What about royalties from your movies?" asked Chase. "You made so many amazing movies. Possibly the best and greatest franchise in the history of cinema."

"Thanks," she said. "I can tell you're a real fan, Detective. But back when I made those movies I wasn't a star at all. I was just a beginning actress and I signed a lousy deal. I got paid twenty-five grand for the first one, a bit more for the others. The last one netted me three hundred thousand."

"Not exactly big money."

"Not exactly. If you subtract taxes, agent fees, social security and all that, there wasn't a whole lot left. Not enough to retire on, that's for sure."

Odelia caught Chase frowning. It was obvious that there was no motive for Zelda to murder Donna. Not if she stood to lose her benefactor. The woman who'd helped her out all these years.

"Are you sure you don't remember where you were yesterday morning, Zelda?" I asked.

She shook her head. "I get these memory lapses. I'll lose hours at a time."

It wasn't hard to figure out why that was. Officers had found Zelda's abandoned car a mile from Donna's house, the door open. Inside, they'd discovered enough weed to supply a small colony. And the smoking thing Dooley and Max had seen her use inside the house wasn't incense but Zelda's bong, which explained the pungent odor that had permeated the house.

"Did Donna also finance your marijuana habit?" she asked.

The woman's eyes widened. "Marijuana? I don't have a marijuana habit."

"Come on, Zelda," said Chase. "We found your car. And your stash."

She sobered. "That's for medicinal purposes only. I have allergies."

"Pot helps with allergies?"

"Pot helps with everything," she said with a lazy grin. "I could actually use some right now. Can you hook me up?"

"Are you really asking a cop to hook you up with drugs?" asked Chase.

She narrowed her eyes. "Is that a trick question?"

He turned to Odelia. "Can I talk to you outside?"

They both left the room. "I don't think she did it," said Chase once they were alone.

"You're only saying that because she's your hero."

He pointed at the woman behind the one-way mirror. "Do you seriously want me to believe that wreck of a human being had the presence of mind to steal a hive of bees, then execute the perfect crime? She doesn't even remember how she got to Donna's house in the first place. Not to mention the fact that Donna paid her rent and who knows what else."

"I was just kidding. I don't think she did it either."

"Oh, Christ!" Chase yelled, fisting his fingers in his hair and pulling. "Back to square one!"

"Looks like it," Odelia confessed. She studied Zelda for a moment, who was now making finger guns and pretending to shoot at the ceiling. Probably reenacting one of the stunts she'd done without a stunt double on the set of *Star Cars*. "We'll just have to keep on digging," she finally said.

"We got the analysis back on some tire tracks we found behind Donna's house."

"And?"

"Toyota Tacoma. We're putting together a list of Tacoma owners. It might take a while."

She nodded. Good old-fashioned police work. Chase was an ace at that kind of thing, and so was her uncle. She depended more on her instincts, her cats and… sheer luck. She rubbed her eyes.

"Why don't you get some sleep?" he suggested. "You look beat."

"Yeah, maybe I'll do that. I could use a few more hours. What about you?"

He smiled. "I'm one of those *Star Cars* dudes, babe. We don't need sleep, only stardust."

She leaned in for a kiss, and that's when something started vibrating in her pocket. Chase reached down and took it out. It was a small black plastic thing, shaped like a rocket. With an expert hand, he switched it off and tucked it back into her pocket, then cocked an inquisitive eyebrow at her.

She blushed. "I'm one of those *Star Rig* gals, babe. We don't need guys, only batteries."

He stroked a finger along her cheek, and huskily said, "Whenever you change your mind about that, you know where to find me."

CHAPTER 27

*O*delia had dropped by the house, announcing that we weren't out of the woods yet. The case, which we'd assumed closed, was still wide open, Zelda Yoke not the cunning killer we'd pegged her as. Bummer. Harriet, returning from her power walk with Brutus, was ecstatic, though.

"I knew it!" she yelled. "I just knew it! No way Max and Dooley caught the killer."

"Why is it so hard to believe we would catch the killer?" I asked, feeling a little offended.

"Because you're boys," said Harriet with amazing lack of logic and reason. "Come on, Brutus. We're leaving."

"But we just got here!" the big, black cat cried. He was lying spread-eagle on the floor, trying to catch his breath.

"And now we're leaving. We have a killer to catch and no time to waste!"

And just when I thought she was going to hit the street and pound the pavement, just like any old-fashioned detective, she hopped up on Odelia's computer table and fired up the computer. With a grunt of despair, Brutus hauled himself up from the floor and shuffled after his ladylove. Glancing over his shoulder, he muttered, "Never get married, fellas. Don't do it." And then he joined Harriet at the computer, ready for another few hours of surfing the web.

Odelia, who'd taken a shower and looked more human when she returned downstairs, said, "Are you guys coming?"

"Nah-uh," said Harriet without looking up from her no doubt strenuous activity. "We're busy trying to find the killer, Odelia. Isn't that right, sugar-pop?"

"Whatever you say, snuggle-cup," said Brutus, having trouble keeping his eyes open.

Odelia stared at the twosome, and for a moment I thought she was going to say something, but then she seemed to think better of it. She turned to us. "What about you guys? Are you coming?"

"Yes, please," I said. Anything to get away from Harriet, who was in a particularly annoying mood today.

We rode in Odelia's pickup to the office, where she dropped us off. "Don't wander off too far," she warned as she locked the car. "And remember about your diet, Max. Don't fall off the wagon."

"I won't," I promised her. We watched her disappear into the offices of the Hampton Cove Gazette and then set foot down the street.

"So where are we going?" asked Dooley.

"Why don't we pay a visit to Kingman?" I suggested. "We haven't seen that cat in a while."

Kingman is Wilbur Vickery's piebald. Wilbur runs the General Store and sells pretty much everything the grown cat needs—and the grown human, for that matter. Dooley must have seen right through me, for he said, "We're just gathering information, right? Not food?"

"Of course! How can you even think about food at a time like this? We have a killer to catch, Dooley, and if we're ever going to beat Harriet at her own game, we need to move fast."

"You don't really think Harriet is ever going to catch the killer by spending time on that computer, do you?"

"I think chances of that happening are slim to none."

We padded over to the Vickery General Store, and found Kingman, perched on the counter, keeping his human company as usual. When he saw us waddling up, he gave us a cheerful salute. "Hey there, fellas. Long time no see. What's happening in your neck of the woods?"

"Oh, nothing special," I said, trying to come across as cool and laidback as Kingman himself.

"Max is on a diet," said Dooley, "and he's not allowed to eat anything other than diet food. So if you were thinking of feeding him some special snack, think again, because if he doesn't stop being morbidly obese he's going to die soon and break Odelia's heart and I'll lose my best friend and I don't think I can take that." He choked up and both Kingman and I looked at the ragamuffin in surprise.

"Dooley," I said. "I had no idea you felt so strongly about this dieting thing."

"I didn't know either," he said in a strangled voice. "Not until Harriet said all that stuff about you dying and all. I don't want you to die, Max. I don't want to lose my best friend in all the world."

"I'm not going to die, buddy. I'm as fit as a horse."

"You're the size of a horse," said Kingman. "Dooley is right. You are too fat for your own good."

I directed a scathing look at him. "How many times do I have to tell you? I'm not fat! I have big bones. It runs in the family."

"You can fool yourself but you can't fool me," said Kingman. "You look just about one sausage away from a massive coronary."

God. If there's one thing I hate it's a cat that has no filter, and Kingman is just such a cat. "All right, all right," I said. "I'll lose weight. I'll slim down until I'm as slim as you."

"Not as easy as it looks," said Kingman. "My body is my temple. I treat it with respect."

"Treat your body with respect, Max," Dooley urged. "If not for yourself, do it for me."

"I already told you I would do the diet thing," I said. "And my word is my bond."

Dooley seemed pleased by this, giving me encouraging pats on the back. "I'm so glad you're finally seeing the light, Max. I can't imagine spending the rest of my life without you."

Ugh. All this sentimentality was seriously getting on my nerves. And then I caught sight of a nice piece of steak that was lying on the floor where someone had dropped it. I looked left. I looked right. Nobody had spotted it. And even without any instigation from me, my paws starting plotting a course to the piece of red steak. I could already feel the texture in my mouth—taste it on my tongue—imagine it sliding down my throat. And I was about to pounce on the delicious morsel when suddenly Dooley entered my field of vision and said, "No, Max. You promised."

"But it's red meat! Red meat is good for me!"

"It's fattening. The last thing you need right now is to fatten up even more."

"I won't fatten up," I told him. "I promise!"

"Eat this and I won't be your friend anymore," Dooley said with uncharacteristic severity.

"Huh?"

"I'm not going to stand idly by and watch you eat yourself to death, Max."

"Well, you don't have to. You just have to watch me eat

that tasty bit of steak." And I made a move to snap it up, only to be forestalled by Dooley once again.

"Choose, Max. Me or that steak."

Phew. Tough choice. Still, instinct is instinct, and red meat is red meat, and I would have gobbled the bit of steak if I suddenly hadn't caught sight of a familiar figure.

"Hey, isn't that Donna's CEO Hillary Davies?"

"I'm not going to fall for that, Max. You're just trying to distract me."

"No, but it really is. Look, she just ran into Donna's ex-husband."

"You'll have to do better than that. You know me, Max. Nothing gets past me."

"Oh, and those must be Donna's kids. Sweetums and Honeychild. Look how Hillary is smiling so sweetly at those kids. It's obvious she's crazy about them."

"Oh, for crying out loud," Dooley said, and grabbed the bit of steak between his teeth and devoured it in one go. He swallowed, then turned to where I was looking.

I stared at him, aghast. "Did you just eat my piece of steak?"

"It wasn't your piece of steak."

"But you just told me it was fattening."

He lifted his chin. "I'm your friend, Max. If I have to sacrifice myself for your sake, I will gladly do so."

I narrowed my eyes at him. "Eating a perfectly delicious and juicy bit of steak doesn't sound like much of a sacrifice to me."

"A friend's gotta do what a friend's gotta do."

And then we both watched as Hillary Davies picked up Sweetums and Honeychild, who turned out to be two adorable apple-cheeked little boys, and hugged them close. Tad Rip watched on with a smile on his face. It was the scene of perfect familial bliss, if not for the fact that it should have been Donna and not her CEO hugging those kids.

"We have to find the killer, Max," said Dooley, obviously sharing my sentiments.

"Yes, we do," I said, and never had I been more resolved to put my best paw forward. Watching Dooley swallow down that tasty sliver of steak I had marked for my own might have had something to do with it as well. I was pretty sure that if we caught the killer, Odelia would be more than happy to buy me not just a tiny piece of steak but a complete slice!

CHAPTER 28

*O*delia was feeling restless. She'd written her article—
what little she knew about the case at this point—
and now there was nothing else to do but go over all the
elements again until something jumped out at her that would
provide the final clue. That moment when everything clicked
into place. And she'd revisited the crime scene in her head
and had gone over all the interviews she and Chase had done
but still nothing took her to that aha moment she was
looking for. Nothing.

Even Max and Dooley were coming up empty, and if
Harriet and Brutus had found something online they weren't
telling, which meant Harriet was probably just surfing to all
the gossip sites as usual.

She looked up when a deferential cough sounded. Her
editor Dan was watching her from the doorway, thoughtfully
rubbing his long white beard. "Stuck, kid?" he asked in his
smoky voice.

"Yeah, pretty much," she admitted.

"You know what I do when I get stuck?"

"Have a smoke?"

"How do you know?"

"I don't smoke, Dan. And I'm not going to start simply because this case doesn't make sense."

"I'm not telling you to smoke, honey. I'm telling you to take a break."

"Take a break?"

"Don't look at me as if I just suggested you to go and harpoon some whales. Taking a break is a perfectly legitimate solution to getting your brain unstuck."

"But I still have a ton of work. There's the county fair, the new addition to the marina, the paddleboard competition—"

"Those can all wait. As your editor what I want you to do right now is to take a break. Get away from your computer for a couple hours and take your mind off things for a while."

"You're a weird editor, Dan," she said. "Most editors prefer to work their reporters to death."

He pointed a stubby, crooked finger at her. "And that's exactly what I don't want you to do. I like you too much to see you work yourself to death, Odelia. And I know from experience that sometimes all you need is some perspective."

"And a break."

"And a break. So shut down that computer of yours, get out of here, and don't let me see you for at least the next couple of hours."

"So what do you suggest I do?"

He threw up his hands. "Go for a walk! Take a swim. Sit on the beach and look at the damned tourists for all I care. But most importantly, don't think about the case!"

Which, as she soon discovered, was easier said than done. She'd gone for a walk, and had walked as far as the boardwalk, taken a seat on one of the benches the town council had been so kind to install, and had stared out across the ocean for a bit. The water was pretty choppy, and kids were squealing happily as they jumped into the cresting waves. And she'd been sitting there for twenty minutes, doing her absolute darndest to empty her mind and NOT think about the case and NOT check her phone, when a deep voice sounded beside her.

"Mind if I join you?"

"Oh, God," she said. "Am I happy to see you."

Chase took a seat next to her on the bench. "Not that I'm not flattered, but any special reason?"

"I've been trying hard NOT to think about the case."

He grinned. "Which is just about the best way to think about the case."

"It is?"

"Of course. What if I tell you NOT to think about pink elephants?"

Suddenly, all she could think about were pink elephants. "I see what you mean."

"Who gave you this sterling piece of advice?"

"Dan. Said if I didn't get out and take a break I was never going to get anywhere."

"Same here," Chase said with a deep sigh. "Only it was your uncle who kicked me out."

"So here we are. Marooned on the beach."

"Yep. You can say that again. So why don't we try NOT talking about the case, huh?"

She laughed. "You're funny, do you know that, Detective Kingsley?"

"You take that back right now," he said with a grin. "Police detectives are not supposed to be funny. It is not in the job description."

"But you're not a detective now, are you? You're on a break, and so am I."

So they sat there for a bit, a convivial silence descending upon them, when suddenly a woman started screaming nearby for help. Immediately, both she and Chase were on their feet.

They reached the woman, who was cradling a little girl in her arms. The girl's breathing was labored and her face deathly pale.

"What happened?" Chase asked urgently.

"She was stung by a bee," the woman wailed.

"She's in shock," Odelia determined. "Did you call 911?"

"I did," said the woman, tears streaming down her face.

Chase checked the girl. "She's not breathing," he said, and immediately started CPR. Odelia took out her phone and called her dad. He just might beat the ambulance. She watched Chase perform the life-saving procedure and when he announced that she was going to be fine, she breathed a sigh of relief and so did the girl's mother. Just then, her dad's car pulled up, and he came hurtling down the stone steps and plowed through the powdery sand until he'd reached them. He was carrying his black doctor's bag and sank down onto his knees next to the girl.

"She was stung by a bee," Odelia told him.

He nodded and went to work. She watched how he took out a needle and proceeded to inject the girl. "Epinephrine," he told the mother. "She went into anaphylactic shock. Has this happened before?"

"No, never. But she's never been stung before either."

"Some people are allergic to bee stings." He carefully monitored the girl's pulse and checked her vital signs. "How do you feel, honey?" he asked when she began to pull through.

She coughed. "I feel nauseous," she said thickly.

"That's normal," he assured her. "As is the swollen tongue and lips. Does your tummy hurt?"

The girl nodded. "Yes, it does."

He smiled at her. "You'll be just fine, darling. What's your name?"

"Jessica."

"I'm Doctor Tex, and you're a very brave girl, Jessica. You're doing great." He turned to Jessica's mother. "She'll feel the effects for a couple of days, but they'll wear off soon enough."

"Oh, doctor," the woman said. "I can't thank you enough."

"Thank my daughter," said Tex. "She's the one who called."

"Thank Chase," said Odelia. "He's the one who performed CPR."

The woman thanked all of them, and gave Chase a big old hug before enveloping her little girl in her arms and smothering her with kisses. "I thought I lost you," she sniffed.

"I'm fine, Mom," Jessica said, embarrassed at the display of affection in front of a bunch of strangers. "It was just a tiny, little prick. Though that bee sting really hurt."

In the distance, the sound of an approaching ambulance could be heard. It pulled up right next to Odelia's dad's car and two paramedics jumped out and made their way over. Odelia and Chase watched as the EMTs gave Jessica a thorough checkup.

"That was a close call," said Chase. "She'd completely stopped breathing for a minute there."

She placed a hand on his arm. "You saved that girl's life, Chase. You're a hero."

"Just doing my duty," he muttered. "Anyone would have done the same."

"Not everyone. Didn't you notice how you were the only one who made an effort?"

"Not many people know CPR," he admitted. "Though probably they should."

Dad joined them, still carrying his little black bag. "She'll be fine," he announced. "Spirited little thing, isn't she?"

"She sure is," Odelia agreed as she watched the girl animatedly talk to the paramedics and the one lifeguard who'd finally decided to put in an appearance. She looked like she was enjoying all this attention, and demanded her mother take a bunch of pictures with her phone.

"Reminds me of something," Dad said.

"Me too. Donna Bruce," Odelia said.

"No, something a colleague once told me. Some woman who wanted to try apitherapy on her daughter, who was suffering from rheumatoid arthritis."

"Apitherapy?" Chase asked.

"Bee sting therapy. The venom of bees purportedly alleviates the effects of the arthritis. Unfortunately the girl turned out to be allergic to bees, just like Jessica over there."

"What happened?" asked Odelia.

"She died. When the mother realized what was going on, she called 911, but too late."

"That's a horrible story," said Chase.

"When was this?"

"Oh, I must have heard this story... about six, seven years ago? I think it was at one of those conferences. There's a lot of bar talk when a bunch of medical professionals get together."

"There's a lot of bar talk when any professionals get together," said Chase. "Or non-professionals for that matter."

For some reason, the story rang a bell with Odelia. "Where did this happen?"

Dad frowned. "I don't remember exactly. I want to say... Cleveland?"

Cleveland... Odelia wondered why this story resonated with her so much, but before she could think things through, the EMTs wandered over and started discussing what happened to Jessica with her dad. She checked her watch and decided it was probably time she headed back to the office. Dan had told her to take a break, but she still had a ton of work to do. Chase seemed to feel the same way, for he asked if he could drop her off somewhere.

As he drove her back to the Hampton Cove Gazette, her mind drifted back to the story her dad had told them. Bees. This whole thing revolved around bees. But how? And why?

CHAPTER 29

We were home again, Dooley and me. We'd done all our usual haunts: the hair salon, the police station, the alleys and back alleys of Hampton Cove, talking to other cats, but they'd yielded no results. On top of that, I was tired. Subsisting on diet food like I did, I tired easily these days and all I wanted was to take a nap and float off into oblivion.

Unfortunately when we walked in through the glass sliding door, Harriet and Brutus were still there, like a couple of unwanted guests you just can't seem to get rid of.

"And? What did you find?" I asked, jumping up onto the couch and settling down in my usual spot.

Harriet merely frowned, as if I'd asked her the wrong question.

"Nothing," Brutus replied in her stead. "Bupkis. Diddly squat. Jack shit."

"Brutus!" Harriet snapped. "Language."

"It's true though, isn't it?" asked Brutus, whose long surfing session seemed to have galvanized him. "I know everything about Justin Bieber's tattoos and even which

188

kidney Selena Gomez had implanted but I still know precious little about who offed Donna Bruce."

Harriet lifted her chin. "We just have to keep on looking. It's only a matter of time before we hit on the telling clue."

"Not by surfing that darned Interweb we won't. How many times can you read about Kim's Paris attack? Seriously, I'm done." And to show us he meant business, he hopped down from the computer table and stretched and yawned.

"Brutus! We're not finished yet."

"I'm sorry, toots. I would tell you I cared about how much weight Mama June lost but I don't."

Harriet's ears colored. "I've been looking at other stuff, too."

"Right. What Honey Boo Boo looks like these days. I'm a cat, honey munch. I don't care about that stuff. What I do care about is treating myself to a nice piece of meat at regular intervals, lounging on the couch with my precious —which is you, by the way—and sneaking around the neighborhood after dark, chasing critters and fighting off trespassers. So if you care to join me—which I sincerely hope you do—you're welcome. If you prefer to find out what the Real Housewives of Nowhereville are up to, that's fine, too. But don't expect me to stick around, cause I won't."

Harriet looked shocked after this unexpected harangue. "Brutus," she muttered brokenly.

"Now what's it gonna be, sugar puss?"

Her blush had deepened. "Brutus, you're suddenly so... dominant."

"A tom's gotta do what a tom's gotta do. Now are you with me or not?"

"Brutus," she breathed, deserting the world of reality TV and dropping down from the computer table. She stalked up to her beau, her tail trembling wildly. "Oh, Brutus…"

Brutus grinned at me and gave me a wink. "Watch and learn, fatso. Watch and learn."

I responded with an eyeroll. So the old Brutus was back, huh? Of course he was. He'd just been suffering from a temporary weakness, as was to be expected.

"We're hitting the town, boys," Brutus announced when Harriet had sidled up to him and was rubbing herself provocatively against his flank. "Don't wait up for us."

And with these words, the revolting couple was off, leaving Dooley and me reeling. Well, Dooley was reeling. I wasn't.

"Why can't I be more like Brutus, Max?" Dooley lamented. "If I could be more like Brutus maybe Harriet would like me too. And then I'd be the one who took her out on the town."

"Do you really want to take Harriet out on the town?"

"Of course I do! She's so..." He sighed forlornly. "... wonderful."

"Oh, Dooley," I muttered, and closed my eyes. I only woke up when something was poking me in the side. I tried to slap it away but the poking only intensified.

"Max! Max, wake up!"

"I'm a cat, Dooley. I'm always awake," I reminded him. Though as a matter of fact I'd actually been sleeping soundly, dreaming of that nice piece of steak Dooley had stolen from me. "What is it?" I finally asked, reluctantly abandoning my dream. If I couldn't eat steak, at least I could dream about it. As far as I know, dreams aren't fattening. Or are they?

"I think I found something," Dooley announced.

"If it's not meat I don't want to know," I muttered, and closed my eyes again.

"It's about Hillary."

"I don't care about politics, Dooley."

When he didn't respond, I opened my eyes again and

found him staring at me. "What do you mean you don't care about politics?"

"Hillary Clinton. Donald Trump. I just don't care."

"Who are Hillary Clinton and Donald Trump?"

"My sentiments exactly. Now leave me be. I have to conserve my strength. I'm on a diet."

"Poor Hillary Davies lost her daughter a couple of years ago."

"She did, huh? That's terrible," I muttered, trying to go back to sleep.

"I was surfing the web, typing in the names of all the suspects in the Donna Bruce murder case and that's what came up."

"Terrible tragedy," I murmured.

"Oh, and they're doing a remake of *Star Cars*, only without Zelda Yoke this time."

"Too bad."

"And Dexter Valdès is writing his autobiography. It's called *Life with a Tiny Wiener*."

"Very tempting."

"And Ransom Montlló is setting up a new version of *A Star is Born*, only this time it's an indie production, made with local talent and featuring Ransom himself and his dog Flea in the lead."

"That's just great. Now if you could just let me—"

"Hey, you guys!" Odelia cried, walking in. "I'm home."

I groaned in agony. Why was it suddenly so hard to get some sleep around here?

"Hey, Odelia," Dooley said with a smile. "I've just discovered a whole new bunch of clues."

Odelia was immediately interested, which just told me how desperate she was. Obviously her investigation was going nowhere, same way ours was. Odelia listened patiently as Dooley rattled off his list of 'clues' while I tried to drown out the droning sound of his voice. Then, suddenly, he must have said something interesting, for Odelia uttered a startled cry and jumped up from the couch like a rocketing pheasant, grabbed her purse and was out the door in a flash. She briefly returned to shout, "You guys just solved this case!" and then she was gone again.

I stared at Dooley, who seemed ecstatic.

"We just solved the case, Max! We solved the case!"

"We did?"

"Didn't you hear Odelia? We found Donna's murderer!"

"So who is it?"

Dooley's exuberance waned. "Um... I don't know."

I shrugged, and went right back to sleep. Humans. They're all nuts.

CHAPTER 30

*O*delia pressed her lips together in a grim expression. She had a pretty good idea what had happened and who was responsible for the murder of Donna Bruce, and as usual her cats had provided her with the telling clue. And as she drove over to Donna's house, the old pickup hurtling along the road and kicking up spray, she pushed the engine to the max. It whined and rattled in protest but she didn't care. She had to reach the house before it was too late and the bird had flown.

A snippet of conversation had drifted back into her memory. Donna's house was going to be put up for sale, her uncle had told her. Tad had no use for it as he was moving back west with the boys after the funeral. The house was going to be emptied out, the most valuable stuff shipped to LA and the rest sold locally or simply thrown away. When she and Chase had found Zelda Yoke asleep in Donna's bed she'd already noticed a lot of stuff was missing, which meant cleanup was well underway. And she knew exactly who was in charge.

When she arrived at the house she saw that the gate was

wide open so she didn't hesitate and drove her pickup up the driveway and parked next to the red Fiat that stood with its rear end backed up to the front door, its trunk open.

She walked up to the house, the thought of calling Chase briefly flitting through her mind. But she wasn't entirely sure her hunch was right, and if it wasn't she didn't want to inconvenience Chase.

She moved into the foyer and called out, "Hello? Anybody here?"

The sound of her voice echoed hollowly in the empty space. They hadn't lost any time, as she saw most of the furniture had already been moved out. She must have just missed the moving crew.

She headed deeper into the house, past the living room and kitchen and into the fitness area. An indoor pool displayed a perfectly tranquil surface, and she could only imagine how many laps Donna must have swum in the chlorinated water. She wouldn't mind owning her own private pool someday, actually. Must be fun to take a swim before breakfast every day.

She took a peek inside the gym, where the equipment had been dismantled and moved out. Only a few loose weights lay around on the floor, and instruction posters for the best posture still decorated the walls. There were even a few posters of Donna in her prime, back when she'd starred in *Car Rigs*. The former actress posed in full star warrior costume, defiantly staring into the camera, a collection of freakishly weird space creatures collected at her feet.

And that's when she heard a noise. It wasn't loud. Just a footfall. She looked up in alarm.

"Hello? I just want a quick word."

She moved toward the back of the private gym and found herself in the sauna space, the wood cabin where Donna had met her end to the right, a few wooden benches placed beneath wooden pegs to her left, several terry bathrobes still dangling from them. She noticed that the door to the sauna was ajar, and wondered if anyone was in there. She took a quick peek but saw that the space was empty. Drawing back, she suddenly heard movement behind her and when she spun around, found herself gazing into the cool blue eyes of Hillary Davies, Donna's trusty CEO.

"Oh, hi, Hillary," she said, quickly recovering from the shock. "I was looking for you."

Hillary smiled. Her head was covered with a scarf and she was wearing coveralls and gloves. "I was just finishing up in here."

"Tad asked you to handle the move?"

"Yes, he did. He didn't want a bunch of strangers rooting through Donna's personal stuff, so he asked me to coordinate the whole shebang. The realtor was in here just now."

"So Tad is selling the place, huh?"

"Yeah, this place and the other one. He never was much of an East Coast guy anyway. I think he's secretly glad he can move back to LA with the boys."

She cleared her throat. "There's something I've been meaning to ask you, Hillary."

The woman raised her eyebrows. "Oh?" She wiped her gloved hand across her nose, leaving a dark smudge.

"You... lost a girl a couple of years ago, isn't that right?"

Hillary nodded. "Suzy. Yeah, we lost her. And then I lost Henry, too."

"Henry?"

"My husband. He couldn't process Suzy's death so he... took his own life shortly after."

"I'm so sorry."

"Yeah." She sniffled, wiping her nose again. "That was a tough time for me. A real tough time."

"She... died after you tried apitherapy to alleviate the consequences of her rheumatic arthritis, right?"

She nodded, blinking now. "She was only ten, but suffering so much. I never even knew kids could get arthritis. Doctors said there wasn't much they could do, and she was in so much pain..."

"And then you read about Donna's apitherapy experiments."

"I got one bee—only one, mind you—just to have a try. Henry wasn't too keen, but I persisted."

"Because Donna advised it."

"Donna.vip has always been my bible. Long before I started to work for her. Donna knows."

"But what Donna didn't know was that bee sting therapy can be very dangerous."

"Even lethal," Hillary said, her voice hoarse now. "One sting, that's all it took." She looked away, swiping at her eyes. "I placed it on her arm with a pair of tweezers, just the way I was supposed to. Henry was working late, and Suzy had been complaining about the pain again, so I decided to give it a try. Suzy was brave—oh, so brave. She said she didn't mind a little prick. She was actually more worried about the bee than herself. Said she didn't want the bee to die, like she read online. The prick was fine. Just a little sting, just like I promised. But then..." She choked. "She had trouble breathing, her throat closing up."

"Probably because her tongue was swollen."

"She looked into my eyes and said the bee had made her dizzy. And then her eyes turned up and she was gone. I—I tried to revive her but I—I couldn't. By the time the ambulance showed up, it was too late. She—she died in my arms. And all from one little bee sting."

"Anaphylactic shock. One sting is enough."

"I didn't know," said Hillary, shaking her head. "The

website… there had been no warning, no instructions on what to do if something went wrong. So…"

"So you blamed Donna Bruce for the death of your girl."

Hillary merely stared at her, eyes wide, face pale.

"You decided that if you could only get close enough to her, you might find a way to make her pay. And you were in luck. She needed a CEO and you had just the right qualifications. So you worked closely with her, trying to figure out how you could get your revenge."

"The woman was totally irresponsible," said Hillary. "She didn't care. All she cared about was making more money and becoming the biggest name in lifestyle advice. When I told her perhaps we should add a disclaimer to the site—at least to the most controversial claims, she laughed me out of the room. Said if people were dumb enough to buy the junk she was peddling, they got exactly what they deserved. That's when I knew she was simply evil."

"So you killed her."

"Yes," said Hillary, her clear blue eyes unwavering. "And I made sure she suffered just as much as Suzy did. And as much as Suzy's mommy and daddy did. I did it for her. And for Henry."

"I understand, Hillary," said Odelia. "And I'm sure that a jury will, too, when they hear the whole story."

The woman frowned. "A jury? What are you talking about?"

"If you come with me now, you can turn yourself in. I'll be there every step of the way."

Hillary laughed. "You can't seriously think I'm going to jail for this."

"You killed someone, Hillary. You didn't think you were going to get away with this, did you?"

"Of course I'm getting away with it. I did what was right. I killed the woman who killed my little girl. Donna got exactly what she deserved, and my only regret is that I didn't do it sooner."

"Donna had two children of her own. I'm sure they won't feel the same way."

Hillary pressed her lips together. "Donna didn't care about those two little brats. All she cared about was herself, and the attention she could get as a mother of two. She used those kids. To her they were nothing more than a PR stunt."

"Let's just—hey!"

Quick as a flash, Hillary gave her such a powerful shove that she fell backwards, tumbling through the open door into the sauna cabin. And before she could get up, the former CEO had slammed the wooden door shut and bolted it from the outside. A sudden sense of panic rose in her chest like bile. She pounded the door. "Let me out! Let me out right now!"

But Hillary merely regarded her coolly, and then she was gone.

"Hey! Hillary!"

She darted an anxious look at the ceiling, hoping the same fate that had befallen Donna wouldn't happen to her. She would hate to be stung to death by a couple thousand bees! When no sound came through the ventilator, she sighed with relief. But then she noticed the temperature in the small space was rising and rising fast. God, no. Hillary had turned up the heat—probably cranked it up to the max! And had turned off the fan.

She tried the door but it was bolted shut. She pounded the one tiny window that offered a view of the outside but it was thick glass, unbreakable without the right tools. She quickly searched her pockets but came up empty. Her purse containing her phone was still in the pickup.

The heat was rising quickly and sweat broke out on her brow. Worse, she was starting to have trouble breathing because of the lack of ventilation. She understood now what Hillary was trying to accomplish. She'd simply let her die from heat exposure. Make it look like an accident. Already she was feeling the strain, and dropped down on the wooden bench. She removed her T-shirt and jeans, and tried to stay calm and collected. Panic wasn't her friend right now—slowing down her heartbeat and helping her body deal with this sudden assault was.

She closed her eyes and tried to remember the few yoga lessons she'd taken. Slow breaths. Centering herself. Someone would come. She'd get through this. She was not going to die.

As the temperature soared, she was now sweating so much her underwear was soaked and she was starting to feel dizzy. And just before she dropped down on the bench, she thought she felt a rush of cool air and a face swimming before her eyes. And then she passed out.

When she came to, she found herself gazing into Chase's eyes. She was lying on the floor and someone was poking at her arm.

"Chase?" she asked weakly. "Where am I? What happened?"

He smiled. "Thank God. I thought I lost you, honey. How are you feeling?"

She smacked her lips. "Thirsty."

He laughed, and when she looked down, she saw that a male nurse was checking her pulse. "She'll be fine," he said. "She's going to need a lot of fluids, though."

"I'll make sure she gets what she needs," Chase assured the man.

She looked around, and saw she was right outside the sauna, the sauna door open. Then memory returned and she tried to sit up. The moment she did, her head started swimming again. "Hillary!" she cried. "Hillary tried to kill me!"

"I know," said Chase, gently easing her down again. "We got her. She's in custody."

"And how is my favorite niece?" asked her uncle, crouching down next to her.

"I'm your only niece," she said weakly.

Her uncle seemed worried. "Please, Odelia, if you don't want me to die from heart failure, never pull a stunt like this again. Next time you want to confront a suspect, call for backup."

"I'm sorry," she said. "I wasn't sure Hillary was the one—though I had my suspicions."

"Good thing Chase had the same suspicions."

She gave Chase a look of surprise. "You did?"

"After what happened on the beach I started looking for the name of that girl from Cleveland. Don't ask me why. A hunch, I guess."

"Women's intuition," she said with a smile. "It's rubbed off on you."

"That might well be the case. Cause that girl turned out to be Hillary's daughter. Died seven years ago after an apitherapy attempt gone wrong. It wasn't a big leap from that incident to Donna's death by bee sting, so…"

"So you flew to my side like a rescuing angel."

"Only a lot uglier," Uncle Alec said with a grin.

Odelia placed her hand on Chase's cheek. "Chase isn't ugly. He's gorgeous."

"That's just the drugs talking," Chase grunted.

"'No, that's me talking. I think you're gorgeous, Detective Kingsley. And I thank you for saving my life."

Uncle Alec shuffled uncomfortably. "I'll give you kids some space," he muttered, and got up.

"The Chief is right, Odelia," said Chase. "Please don't pull a stunt like this again. Next time call me first."

"I will," she promised him. "And my cats, of course."

"Of course. Where would we be without your cats?"

"Nowhere! They solved this whole thing! Well, Dooley did, at least."

"Of course he did. Let's get you out of here. You're not making any sense."

He helped her to her feet and she leaned on him as they walked away from that fateful sauna cabin. She noticed someone had dressed her in a thick sweater. Since it said NYPD on the front she assumed it was Chase's. "What happened to my bra and panties? They must have been soaked."

"I… removed them," he said, blushing slightly. "But I looked away as I did."

"Of course you did," she said, placing her hand on his chest and squeezing.

"Now what was that about me being a gorgeous rescuing angel again?" he asked when they were out in the open, and making their way to his car.

"Oh, you liked that, didn't you?"

"It's not something I hear every day."

"Well, if you propose to me, Chase Kingsley, I promise I will tell you all that and more."

He eyed her sternly. "Still the drugs talking. Let's get you to your father."

"Yes, because you'll have to ask his approval. He's old-fashioned he is, my dad."

"Ask for his approval, huh?"

"Yep. Ask for his daughter's hand in marriage."

"And if he doesn't approve?"

"Then you're shit out of luck, buster."

He laughed. "Now I know it's the drugs talking."

"I'm serious!"

"So am I. Let's get you home and into your jammies."

"Ooh. Naughty naughty, Detective."

Unfortunately, the moment she stepped into his car, she passed out again. She had a dim recollection of Chase carrying her up the stairs and tucking her into bed. He pressed a kiss to her brow, hoisted Max onto the bed and then she fell into a well-deserved sleep.

EPILOGUE

When I finally looked up from my bowl, I was feeling extremely pleased with myself. In the days that had passed since Odelia had caught Donna's killer, I'd stuck to my diet and Dooley had stuck to his. And as I had slimmed down, Dooley had packed on the pounds. It was probably too much to say we were the same weight, but we were a lot closer in size than before. Dooley would always be a skinny cat, of course, and me a more sizable one, but I liked to think we'd both benefited from this uncomfortable episode in our lives.

When Chase had brought Odelia home, half unconscious, it had come as quite a shock to us, and when I'd seen her like that, I'd sworn that I was going to lose those pounds no matter what. We'd obviously let our human down in her hour of need and I was feeling very badly about it, even though Odelia said there was nothing we could have done.

I still felt that if I'd been more alert, we would never have allowed her to go off without her feline assistants by her side. I needed to be fitter, healthier and stronger than ever, if I was going to be my human's protector, and for some strange reason all of a sudden I didn't feel so hungry again all the time, or so weak. And even the diet food suddenly tasted better.

Which just goes to show: it's all a matter of psychology. I once saw that on the Discovery Channel, so it must be true.

It was barbecue time at the Pooles again, and for the occasion Odelia had placed four bowls in a row, our names printed on the sides: Max, Dooley, Harriet and Brutus. The fearsome foursome. And for the first time in days, I wasn't eating diet kibble but an actual piece of red meat!

All the usual suspects were present and accounted for: Tex and Marge, Vesta, Uncle Alec, Odelia and Chase. After we'd eaten our fill, us cats jumped up on the porch swing and settled in for the evening, watching our humans eat. Watching humans is actually one of my favorite hobbies, apart from cat choir and snooping around, of course.

Odelia wandered over, a Coke Zero in her hand. "And? How was the food?"

"Delicious," I said. "Though I don't feel like I deserve it."

"Oh, stop it, Max," she said with a smile. "You guys cracked this case."

"No, Dooley did," I said honestly. "I just slept right through the whole thing."

"You all worked together, just like you're supposed to. And I'm very proud of you. All of you."

"You are?" asked Harriet, who'd been feeling kinda bummed out at the role she'd played. Or not played.

"Yes, I am. You guys are a real team. My fierce feline team."

"Talking to your cats again?" Chase asked, ambling up.

Odelia turned to him. "Of course I am. I'm crazy cat lady, remember?"

"You're my lady," he said huskily, and took her in an embrace. Smooching ensued, and cheers rang out from

Odelia's family. It was safe to say this burly cop was a big hit with the Poole clan.

Just then, a skinny, pimply UPS guy arrived in their midst, and asked, "Vesta Muffin? Who's Vesta Muffin?"

"Oh, God. Not again," Tex muttered.

"That's me," said Gran. "Right here, buddy." She took reception of a small package and signed off on it. And then she went and handed it to… Marge. "Here you go, honey. This is for you."

Marge gave her mother a look of surprise. "For me? Are you sure?"

"Yes, I am. And I even paid for it with my own money."

Marge opened the package, and discovered it contained a pair of gold hoops. "Mom!"

Gran nodded. "Just my way of apologizing for all that hoopla with the bees."

Mom wiped away a tear and took her mother in an embrace. "I love you, Mom."

"And I love you, honey. Thanks for putting up with me all these years. I know it can't have been easy."

Us cats also wiped away tears. Humans. They can really surprise you sometimes.

And as the Pooles sat down for dinner, Marge showing off her gold hoops and Tex showing off his barbecue skills, Uncle Alec and Chase discussed the case and Gran… was carefully looking around, then, when she was sure no one was watching, took the box that had contained Marge's hoops and retrieved it. And as she stalked off towards the house, I thought I could hear a definite buzzing sound coming from inside that box. When she saw four cats watching her every move, she pressed her finger to her lips. "Not a word, all right?" she whispered, and disappeared inside.

Humans. They're completely bananas. Or is it beeneenees?

"So Dooley cracked this case, huh, Max?" asked Brutus. "And you slept right through it."

I might have admitted this to Odelia but I wasn't going to admit it to Brutus. "Dooley cracked this case but he had a lot of help from me," I said therefore.

"Max is right," said Dooley. "I could never have done it without him."

"But you're the one who discovered that telling bit about the bees, right?" Brutus insisted.

I saw where he was going with this. "Let me stop you right there, Brutus," I said. "I was the one who taught Dooley how to surf the web, so technically I'm the one who discovered that clue."

"Horse manure," Brutus growled. "You admitted yourself you were passed out on the couch at the time while Dooley did all the heavy lifting. He's the real hero here. Isn't that right, Harriet?"

Harriet was otherwise engaged, though, as she sat staring out at the hedge at the end of the garden. "Mh?" she asked finally, when Brutus nudged her. "Oh, you're right, smooching partner. Dooley solved this case. He won fair and square."

"It wasn't a contest," Dooley muttered, eyeing me uncertainly. "You heard Odelia. We all worked together. Played our part. We're a real team. Odelia's fierce feline team."

"But you played a bigger part than the rest of us," Brutus said. "So you should get the credit."

"Oh, I don't know…"

Brutus slapped him on the back and Dooley hiccuped. "Sherlock Dooley. Got a nice ring to it."

"I was just messing about online," Dooley said nervously. "No biggie."

"You made us all look good, buddy. Respect."

"Thanks. I guess."

"And you, Max, have completely lost your touch. I think it's all that weight loss. It's affected your brain. I knew this would happen."

"You did?" I asked, wondering where he was going with this.

"Sure. You lose weight, you lose brain cells. And you, my friend, have lost so much weight you must have lost half of your brain. It's a miracle you can still think straight. Quick, how much is nine divided by three?"

"T-three?"

He grinned at me. "You weren't sure, were you? Admit it, Max. Your brain resembles a big chunk of cheese. Swiss cheese. With a big bunch of holes in it. More holes than cheese."

I gulped, the vivid picture Brutus was painting affecting me powerfully. "You think?"

"Of course!" He shook his head sadly. "Good thing Dooley's brain is as sharp as ever, or else Odelia would have to trade you in for a new model. Can't have a cat sleuth with Swiss cheese for a brain."

He was right, of course. I had been feeling a little weak lately. And after allowing Odelia to walk off into danger like that, it was obvious I was slipping and slipping badly.

"Don't listen to him, Max," said Dooley. "Your brain is fine."

"But I have lost a lot of weight," I said, gesturing at my flabby belly.

"Brains aren't muscles," Dooley said.

"Are you sure?"

He hesitated. "Reasonably."

I shivered from head to toe. I could see my brain shrinking even more. Soon there would be nothing left!

"You know what I'll do?" asked Brutus.

"What?"

"Just out of the goodness of my heart, mind you."

"What is it?"

"From now on why don't I assume a leadership role in this small outfit of ours?"

I found myself nodding even before he'd finished the sentence. "Maybe you're right."

"Dooley will be the brains of the operation—obviously. Harriet will be the pretty face. And I will run the outfit."

"And me?" I asked in a feeble voice.

He eyed me sternly. "Why don't I appoint you my assistant?"

"I would like that," I said, still thinking about my cheesy brain. "But do you think I'm up to the task?"

"We'll just have to wait and see," he said. "Somehow I doubt it, Maxie baby, but I'm willing to take a chance on you. That's the kind of cat I am. Kind-hearted and generous to a fault. Isn't that right, babe?"

Harriet, still focused on the end of the garden, murmured her assent.

"What are you looking at, sweet cakes?" Brutus asked, annoyed now.

But Harriet didn't respond. Instead, she jumped down from the swing and picked her way along the humans, who were all gathered around Doctor Tex, toasting his lovely wife Marge.

"What's the matter with Harriet?" asked Dooley.

We followed Harriet with our eyes, and when she finally reached the hedge, she plunked down on her haunches and just sat there. At least, that's what I thought. When I looked closer, I saw her lips were moving. She was talking to someone, and that someone was partially obscured by the boxwood hedge.

"Oh, my God," said Dooley.

"What? What?!" Brutus cried.

"It's… Diego."

We all goggled at the scene, and when the orange cat finally emerged from the hedge, and rubbed noses with Harriet, we all gasped in shock.

Our mortal enemy Diego had returned.

"What do we do?" asked Dooley, panicking. "Brutus? What do we do?!"

But Brutus, our newly self-appointed leader, had been struck dumb. Finally, he turned to me. "Max!" he bleated like a sickly sheep. "What do we do?"

"But I thought you were our leader!"

"I can't be the leader! This is Diego we're talking about! And he's stealing my woman! Again!"

"Well, I can't be the leader. I have Swiss cheese for a brain!"

"I was just joshing you! Your brain is fine!"

"See?" asked Dooley. "Brains aren't muscles. They're… something else."

A feeling of resolve stole over me as I regarded Diego, who'd casually draped a paw across Harriet's shoulder and was looking more smug than ever. Then I said, "Winter is coming, fellas."

"What does that even mean?!" Brutus cried, desperately shaking his paws.

I shrugged. "No idea. But it's got a nice ring to it, doesn't it?"

Just then, Diego blew us a kiss, his face splitting into a particularly cheeky grin.

Brutus, Dooley and I watched him stoically. This meant war.

EXCERPT FROM PURRFECT RIVALRY (THE MYSTERIES OF MAX 6)

Chapter One

I woke up from a sudden chill and discovered I'd fallen asleep on the kitchen floor again. In spite of my protective layer of belly muscle insulating me against the cold, I was freezing. The first thing that occurred to me was the startling observation that the reason for my vigil—the protection of my bowl of food—had been for naught: the bowl was empty!

I quickly trotted over and gasped. To my horror, all three of my bowls had been emptied overnight: the one containing my extra-crunchy vitamin-enhanced prime-brand kibble, the one with my extra-yummy Cat Snax, and even the one with my purified fresh water, which Odelia makes sure is filled to the brim every evening before she retires to bed.

I groaned in dismay. I knew whodunit, of course. It was the whole reason I'd started my nocturnal kitchen vigil. To protect my food supply. And now my stash had been raided. Just like it had been raided the night before, and the night before and the night before that!

Gah. This was getting ridiculous.

Chilled to the bone—a condition exacerbated by the kitchen door being ajar, another irksome habit of the food thief—I decided to warm myself in Odelia's bed. I padded out of the kitchen into the living room and then up the stairs. The sun was already making a valiant attempt to hoist itself over the horizon and would soon be casting the world in its golden hue. Time for Odelia to wake up, and for me to enjoy the best part of the day: my daily snuggle with my human, my nose pressed into her armpit while I purred up a storm and she cuddled me and made me happy to be alive.

This morning, as Odelia gently returned to the land of wakefulness, I made up my mind to have a heart-to-heart talk with her about the state of affairs at the house, and tell her straight out about my long list of grievances. She needed to get rid of the vile serpent she'd nursed at her unsuspecting bosom for far too long.

Odelia is a sweetheart. Too sweet for her own good. It was time to point a damning finger at the horrible pest who'd invaded our lives and allow things to go back to normal.

I trudged up the stairs and with some effort arrived at the top. Crossing the landing, I set paw for her room, then glanced up at the bed. Odelia sleeps in one of those boxspring contraptions, and navigating the jump onto the bed has lately proven something of a challenge. Since Odelia put me on a diet things have improved, and I now made the jump without a hitch, and more or less gracefully landed on all fours on the foot of the bed.

My human was still sleeping peacefully, her even breathing indicating she didn't have a care in the world. My heart warmed and a smile slid up my furry face. Odelia might be misguided, she's the kindest and most decent human I know, and I actually looked forward to pressing my wet and cold nose to her side and basking in the warmth of her embrace.

And I was just about to join her when I discovered to my extreme horror and dismay that a smallish orange cat had beaten me to the punch and had wriggled himself into Odelia's arms, enjoying an embrace that was rightfully mine! Diego! He'd taken my spot!

Even as I was gawking at the spectacle, my mouth opening and closing a few times in helpless fury, the foul usurper opened his eyes and gave me an insolent stare with those slate gray eyes of his, as if to say: whatcha gonna do about it, buddy?

And then he produced the most triumphant grin any cat has ever produced since cats have found it in their generous hearts to give humans the benefit of their company.

"Hey, doofus. Finally decided to wake up, huh? I thought for sure you passed out."

"I wasn't passed out. I was sleeping," I indignantly told the orange menace.

"Sure, sure. Whatever you say, bud," Diego said, and then closed his eyes again, nestling deeper into Odelia's embrace.

Her long blond tresses were spread out across the pillow, and Diego, without a doubt the foulest cat who's ever lived, eagerly dug his face into her hair, just the way I like to do, and breathed in her delicious human scent, a wicked smile spreading across his features.

"Hey," I hissed, reluctant to wake Odelia up. "That's my spot! You stole my spot!"

Diego smirked. "And now it's mine. Got a problem with that, fatso?"

My teeth came together with a click. "For your information, I'm not fat. I'm big-boned. It runs in my family. And yes, I do have a problem with that. Just like I have a problem with the fact that you ate all of my food! And that you left the door open again last night!"

"My food, you mean. And why wouldn't I eat it? Odelia put it out for me."

"It's my food and you know it! She puts out separate bowls for you and for me and you ate everything—my food *and* yours!"

"You know what, Max? I think it's time you and I laid down some ground rules. I mean, if we're going to be living together and all we need to set some boundaries."

I liked the sound of that. "Okay. First rule: don't touch my food. Second rule: don't use my litter box. Third rule: don't snuggle up to Odelia in the morning. That's my job and she hates it when other cats take over from me. I've got that extra-special snuggle she likes which, along with my extra-special purrs, puts her in a good mood for the rest of the day."

"I like your rules, Max. They seem more than fair. Which is why I'm only going to make a few slight emendations. First rule: your food is now my food. Second rule: your litter box is now my litter box. Third rule: Odelia prefers my brand of snuggles so your morning cuddle time is now my morning cuddle time." He gave me a wink. "Thanks for listening."

At this, clearly feeling he'd said what he had to say without inclination to elaborate, he closed his eyes and burrowed deeper into Odelia's armpit, purring up a storm.

To my not inconsiderate consternation, Odelia actually started stroking his fur!

Diego opened one eye as if to say, 'See? My extra-special snuggles hit the spot.'

I would have hit a spot on his head had I been less of a gentlecat. Instead, I gave Odelia a soft nudge, then, when she still refused to wake up, resorted to my trademark kneading technique: placing both front paws on her stomach and pretending it was a piece of dough that needed to be persuaded into perfect consistency and shape. And when that still didn't give me the result I was looking for, I added some claw for that extra oomph you want.

Odelia opened first one seaweed-green eye and then the other, and finally a smile spread across her features. "Max. Diego. So nice to see you guys getting along so well."

I would have lodged a formal protest had she not invited me into the crook of her right arm, even while Diego occupied the crook of her left, and soon I was purring away.

Diego might have tried to take my place in Odelia's heart, just like he'd taken my place in her home and my litter box, but it was obvious that my human still cared about me, and soon my frigid bones were warmed up again, and so was my wounded heart.

Chapter Two

Having woken up with not one but two cats in her arms, Odelia Poole started the new day with a smile and the distinct impression she was truly blessed.

She'd been slightly anxious when Diego entered their lives again—it's always a tough proposition for a cat to accept the introduction of a second cat into his home—but she now felt that Max was adjusting wonderfully. Soon he and Diego would be best buddies, exchanging high-fives and chasing mice together—or whatever it was that buddy cats did.

She displaced both felines, drawing a disappointed mewling sound from Max, and slid from between the covers. She placed both feet into her bunny slippers and shuffled over to the window and threw the curtains wide, allowing the sun to stream into the bedroom.

Gazing out across her modest domain—the small patch of

backyard that she called her own—she reveled for a moment in the pleasant sound of birdsong and saw that a tiny sparrow was sitting in the top of a beech tree and was singing at the top of its tiny lungs.

"A private serenade," she murmured, enchanted. "Much obliged, good sir or lady."

She rubbed her eyes, then stretched and yawned cavernously. Shuffling out of her room, only half awake, she picked her way along the stairs. Before she'd imbibed a decent amount of caffeine, she usually felt as if she'd much rather still be in bed, even though her mind had decided she should kickstart her day. As the intrepid—and only— reporter for the Hampton Cove Gazette she had things to do, people to meet and articles to write.

She started the coffeemaker and rummaged around in the fridge and kitchen cupboards for something edible when she became aware of a marked chill in the air.

Searching around for the source of the cold front that had rolled in, she saw that the kitchen door was ajar. She urgently needed to install a pet door, so Max and Diego wouldn't keep pushing open the door in the middle of the night. There had been a spate of break-ins lately, and holding an open house day in and day out perhaps wasn't such a good idea.

Not that she had a lot of valuables to steal—or other stuff sneak thieves would be remotely interested in. One simply cannot amass a wealth of material possessions on a reporter's salary. But still. No sense in giving them easy access to her home and hearth.

She made a mental note to talk to her dad. Then, discovering she was out of cereal, milk and yogurt, decided not to postpone the urgent missive but deliver it in person.

So she slipped her feet into the galoshes she kept by the

kitchen door, cinched her pink terry cloth robe tighter around her slight frame, and stepped out into the backyard.

Since her parents lived next door, and a convenient opening in the hedge that divided the respective backyards provided easy access, she arrived at her final destination in seven seconds flat, without breaking a sweat, cup of coffee in hand, taking occasional sips.

The hits of caffeine drove the sleep from her body, and by the time she was opening her parents' screen door and stepping into their kitchen, she was more or less human again.

"Hey, sweetie," said her mother, who was pouring herself a cup of coffee. "You're early."

"Ran out of breakfast essentials," she intimated, and started foraging the fridge. Juice, milk, yogurt… Check, check and check. She took a bowl from the cupboard over the sink, dragged down the oversized box of Corn Flakes, and started her own breakfast prep.

Her mother, who was the spitting image of Odelia, albeit with a touch of gray streaking her own blond hair, called out, "Tex, honey! Breakfast is ready!"

Taking a seat at the kitchen counter, Odelia quickly dug in, alternating between scooping up her cereal, now soaked in milk and drowned in fruit yogurt with half a banana, and sipping from her coffee, to which her mother now added creamer and a spoon of sugar.

"How are things going at the paper?" asked her mom, taking a seat at the counter.

"Great. I still have that article to finish about the new school play and the upcoming senior citizen dance—and I'm still hoping to get lucky and land that exclusive one-on-one with the one and only Charlie Dieber!"

"Ooh. Aren't you the lucky one?"

"Yeah. So far Dan struck out with Charlie's management,

but I'm hoping they change their minds. Keeping my fingers crossed!"

Mom crossed her fingers and so did Odelia. They were both equally big Dieber fans.

Odelia's father, who'd entered the kitchen, asked, "Dieber. Isn't he that actor—"

"Singer, Dad."

"Right. I knew that."

Tex Poole was a large man, with a shock of white hair and an engaging smile. He was digging around the cupboards, opening door after door, until Mom said, "Food's on the table, hon."

He glanced down at the bowl of oatmeal porridge Mom had placed on the counter and grimaced. "It's at times like these that I sincerely regret attending medical school. Why couldn't I have become a plumber, and be blissfully unaware of the importance of diet?"

Mom waved a hand. "Even plumbers have to watch their cholesterol levels. No more saturated fats for you. Those levels need to come down and they need to come down before you go and have a stroke or some other horrible incident I don't even want to think about."

"Yeah, Dad," said Odelia. "Even plumbers need to look after their pipes."

"Ha ha. I never knew I raised a comedian for a daughter." He plunked down, staring at the distasteful-looking sludge, spoon raised but not making any indication to start eating it.

"Here, have some of my yogurt," Odelia said, feeling sorry for her dad, who'd been forced to put himself on a diet after discovering his cholesterol levels were off the charts.

He gratefully added some yogurt to his porridge, took a deep breath and dug in. "I know this stuff is healthy—but why does it have to taste so bad?"

"You'll get used to it," Mom said.

"Oh, Dad, if you have time, could you install a pet door over at my place?"

"I'll do it today," said her father, visibly quivering when the first spoon of oatmeal hit his esophagus and the gloop proceeded to slide down his gullet and into his stomach.

"Wasn't it today that Charlie Dieber was on Morning Sunshine?" asked Mom.

"Oh! Right! Better turn on the TV," she instructed her mother.

Mom obligingly switched on the TV set, but the story featured on the televised radio show was an item about freshly hatched chicks, and Odelia quickly lost interest.

"Looks like we just missed it," said Mom.

Just then, Odelia's grandmother waltzed into the kitchen, holding her new iPhone to her ear, and nodding seriously. "Yes, Your Holiness. But there are children dying in Angujistan every day, and we need to get a handle on the situation before things get out of hand."

Odelia exchanged a puzzled look with her mother, who merely rolled her eyes.

"Yes, Pope Francis," said Gran as she took a seat at the counter and gestured at her empty cup that read, 'Greatest Grandma in the World.' Odelia poured coffee into the cup while Gran continued her curious conversation. "Yeah, I agree we can do more, Your Holiness. Have you thought about getting in touch with the United Nations or UNICEF? I would advise you to get on the horn with Ban Ki-moon pronto, Francis. Just tell him what I just told you." Her wrinkled face creased into a wide smile. "No, *you're* welcome, Your Holiness. Us Catholics have to stick together. Yes, just doing my part for world peace."

She disconnected, placed her iPhone on the table and took a sip of coffee. Only then did she notice that the rest of her family were intently staring at her.

"What?" she asked. "Never heard a woman chat with the Pope before?"

"You were actually chatting with the pope just now?" asked Odelia. "*The* pope?"

"The one in Rome?" asked Dad, gratefully using this interruption as an excuse to put down his spoon.

Gran shook her head, causing her tiny white curls to dance around her wrinkly features. "Do you know any other popes? Of course the one in Rome. I told Francis he needs to get a handle on this Angujistan business before more people die and he agreed wholeheartedly. As he should. When a fellow Catholic calls in with an urgent message it's only natural that he would be thrilled. He told me he'd heed my most excellent advice."

"Your grandmother has been advising world leaders," said Mom at Odelia's unposed question. "She's already talked to Bong Si-moon."

"Ban Ki-moon," Gran was quick to correct her.

"That one. He runs the United Nations."

"Great guy," said Gran. "Very happy to chat."

"And who was that other one you talked to?" asked Mom.

"Try to keep up, Marge. Bill Gates. Sharp dude. We talked about providing housing for the poor. I gave him a few suggestions and he was more than happy to jot them down."

Dad gave Odelia a knowing look. "We're in the presence of greatness, Odelia."

"Yeah, forget about Charlie Dieber," Mom added. "It's your grandmother you should be interviewing."

"But how?" Odelia asked. "How do you get in touch with these people?"

Gran shrugged. "I have my ways." She hopped from the stool with surprising agility. "Gotta be going. I'm expecting a call from the President. Give him a piece of my mind."

And with these words, she stalked off, frowning at her

phone and very much looking the part of the highly regarded proficient advisor to the world's political and business elite.

Odelia was going to ask her parents what the heck was going on, but Mom shushed her and turned up the volume on the TV set. As they watched, the host announced with breathless relish that shots had been fired at Charlie Dieber as he exited the studio. Visibly disappointed, the radio jockey clarified that Charlie was unharmed and that his bodyguard had sustained the brunt of the attack and had been pronounced dead at the scene.

"Sweet Jesus!" Mom cried, pressing her hands to the sides of her head. "Thank God Charlie lives!"

"Poor bodyguard, though," Odelia said, shaking her head.

"Yeah, imagine having to take a bullet for Charlie Dieber," Dad quipped.

Mom shut him up with a pointed look. "The man died so Charlie could live. He's a hero and a saint and should be praised for his brave and selfless act."

Dang. Mom was an even bigger Bedieber than Odelia would have guessed.

She promptly got up. "This is big," she announced. "I have to get over there and break this story."

"And while you're at it don't forget to ask for Charlie's autograph, honey," Mom said as she moved to the door.

"If I get within ten feet of Charlie I'm not going to nag him about autographs, Mom."

"You promised!" she called out after her.

"That was before someone tried to drill a hole in him!"

Chapter Three

We were seated in Odelia's backyard, me, Dooley and Brutus, for an emergency meeting. Hidden behind the gardenias, from time to time ducking our heads up to see if the coast was clear and we weren't being overheard, we conducted our meeting with the stealth and solemnity the situation demanded. We were at war, and it was all paws on deck.

"He ate all your food?" asked Dooley. The gray Ragamuffin looked shocked.

"Everything. Every last morsel," I confirmed.

"That's not very nice."

"Not nice?! It's downright criminal!"

"You can have some of my food," Dooley magnanimously offered. "There's plenty."

"Yeah, have some of mine, too," said Brutus, a powerfully built black cat who'd been my mortal enemy until not all that long ago. In fact the arrival of Diego had created a bond between us that had wiped out our former enmity and turned us into unlikely allies instead.

"Will you look at that?" Dooley asked, a somber note in his voice.

We peeked through the gardenias and Brutus drew in a sharp breath when he saw Diego seated on the terrace with Harriet, pressing their paws together in a cloying picture of loved-up cuteness. Any moment Celine Dion could burst into the *Titanic* theme song.

"Don't look, Brutus. Just don't look," I advised the cat, who'd been Harriet's beau before Diego's fateful return.

But Brutus couldn't tear his eyes away from the train wreck even if he wanted to. Nor could I, actually, or Dooley, who'd also been one of Harriet's admirers. In fact it was safe to say I was probably the only male feline for miles around who'd never been into the white Persian. No idea why that was. Probably the fact that she was one of those haughty specimens, who enjoyed lording it over other cats, a quality that set my teeth on edge.

"This is too much," growled Brutus. "Stealing your food. Stealing my girlfriend—"

"Stealing my litter box and my morning cuddle with Odelia," I said somberly.

They gawked at me. "He uses your litter box?" asked Brutus. "Say it isn't so, Max!"

I nodded in confirmation. "Sadly, yes. I've been forced to do my business in Odelia's rhododendrons ever since Diego's return. No way am I going to suffer the indignation of relieving myself in a place that reeks of Diego. Talk about suffering the ultimate humiliation."

Brutus and Dooley sat in stunned silence, as they imagined having to share a litter box with Diego. This was bad, their silence seemed to indicate. This was extremely bad.

"Did you say he stole your morning cuddle with Odelia?" asked Dooley.

"He did." I proceeded to describe my shock and dismay when I discovered Diego snuggling up to Odelia that morning. How he didn't even bat an eye when I confronted him.

"Oh, the horror," muttered Brutus. "The heartbreak. The infuriating gall of the cat!"

"We have to do something about this, you guys," I said. "I feel like he's slowly but surely trying to get rid of me. Before I know it, Odelia will vote Diego Most Valuable Cat."

"Odelia would never do that," said Dooley, eyes wide. "Would she?"

"I wouldn't be surprised if Diego is trying to poison Odelia's mind," said Brutus.

I stared at him. "Poison Odelia? But why?"

"Poison her mind—set her against you."

"No way," Dooley gasped. "There's just no way!"

"Oh, yes, there is," Brutus assured him. "He'll feed her all kinds of lies. Start with something innocuous, like the fact that Max left some poop on the floor, for instance."

Dooley turned to me. "Max! Did you poop on the floor?"

"Of course I didn't poop on the floor! He's talking about Diego."

"Diego pooped on the floor?!"

"Oh, Dooley," I said. "Try to pay attention."

"*Diego* could poop on the floor," Brutus explained, "and then tell Odelia *Max* did it."

The pure deviousness of the scheme seemed to shock Dooley, for he audibly gasped.

"And when she's finally had enough, she'll get rid of Max," Brutus continued.

"Get rid of me!"

Brutus nodded somberly. "The animal shelter, Max. Where all cats go to die."

"Noooo!"

"Oh, yes. Mark my words. Before you know it, you'll be locked up in a cage the size of a shoebox, waiting to be gassed or whatever it is that they do at these establishments."

I sank back on my haunches, the terrible fate that awaited me suddenly looming large and ominous. "I don't want to go to the shelter, you guys. I don't want to be gassed!"

"You might get an injection," Brutus said. "I've heard some even offer electrocution."

His words provided no comfort. I'd suffered injections from Vena Aleman, Odelia's go-to veterinarian. And I'd seen *The Green Mile.* No electrocution for me, thank you very much.

"We have to stop him," I said, a tremor in my voice. "We have to do something."

"Before Diego poops on the floor," Dooley added, his mind stuck on that image.

"Then let's get rid of this pest," said Brutus, pointing a resolute claw at Diego.

"But how? We tried to get rid of him before, remember? He's hard to dislodge."

"There's only one cat in this town who's ever managed to get rid of Diego," said Brutus, "and that's Clarice. We have to find her and convince her to repeat the procedure."

"I remember," I said, cheering up a little. Clarice is a feral cat, Hampton Cove's very own dumpster-diving feline superhero, swatting away lesser cats with a flick of her paw and putting the fear of God into everyone she meets. Even though I'm scared stiff of her—and so are Dooley and Brutus—she's helped us out on more than one occasion, and even received a standing invitation from Odelia to raid her supply of cat food any time she wants. Not that she ever shows her whiskers around here. She prefers to traipse through the woods that surround our small hamlet, roaming around unfettered like the maverick cat that she is.

"Brutus is right, Max," said Dooley. "Clarice is our only hope."

"I don't know," I said. "Last time she drove him away he quickly returned. What's to make him stay away now? And who's to say Clarice will want to do our dirty work for us?"

"Max is right, Brutus," said Dooley. "Clarice takes orders from no one."

"We're not going to order her around," said Brutus. "We'll ask her nicely. In exchange for a lifetime supply of Cat Snax I'm sure even she can be persuaded to do the right thing."

"Brutus is right, Max," said Dooley. "No one says no to a lifetime supply of Cat Snax."

"Clarice is going to need more than Cat Snax. You guys, we're talking about a cat who feeds on mice and rats and who knows what else. This is a raw foodie—not a pampered pet."

"Max is right—"

"Oh, shut up, Dooley," Brutus growled. "So we'll offer her

raw meat—I don't care. If I have to I'll catch her some nasty, hairy rats myself. *Anything* to get rid of that horrible pest." He turned a vicious eye on Diego, who was now exchanging tender smooches with Harriet, and lowered his voice to a menacing snarl. "That cat's got to go, before I commit felinicide."

ALSO BY NIC SAINT

Nora Steel

Murder Retreat

The Kellys

Murder Motel

Death in Suburbia

Emily Stone

Murder at the Art Class

Washington & Jefferson

First Shot

Alice Whitehouse

Spooky Times

Spooky Trills

Spooky End

Spooky Spells

Ghosts of London

Between a Ghost and a Spooky Place

Public Ghost Number One

Ghost Save the Queen

Box Set 1 (Books 1-3)

A Tale of Two Harrys

Ghost of Girlband Past

Ghostlier Things

Charleneland

Deadly Ride

Final Ride

Neighborhood Witch Committee

Witchy Start

Witchy Worries

Witchy Wishes

Saffron Diffley

Crime and Retribution

Vice and Verdict

Felonies and Penalties (Saffron Diffley Short 1)

The B-Team

Once Upon a Spy

Tate-à-Tate

Enemy of the Tates

Ghosts vs. Spies

The Ghost Who Came in from the Cold

Witchy Fingers

Witchy Trouble

Witchy Hexations

Witchy Possessions

Witchy Riches

Box Set 1 (Books 1-4)

The Mysteries of Bell & Whitehouse

One Spoonful of Trouble

Two Scoops of Murder

Three Shots of Disaster

Box Set 1 (Books 1-3)

A Twist of Wraith

A Touch of Ghost

A Clash of Spooks

Box Set 2 (Books 4-6)

The Stuffing of Nightmares

A Breath of Dead Air

An Act of Hodd

Box Set 3 (Books 7-9)

A Game of Dons

Standalone Novels

When in Bruges

The Whiskered Spy

ThrillFix

Homejacking

The Eighth Billionaire

The Wrong Woman

ABOUT NIC

Nic Saint is the pen name for writing couple Nick and Nicole Saint. They've penned 70+ novels in the romance, cat sleuth, middle grade, suspense, comedy and cozy mystery genres. Nicole has a background in accounting and Nick in political science and before being struck by the writing bug the Saints worked odd jobs around the world (including massage therapist in Mexico, gardener in Italy, restaurant manager in India, and Berlitz teacher in Belgium).

When they're not writing they enjoy Christmas-themed Hallmark movies (whether it's Christmas or not), all manner of pastry, comic books, a daily dose of yoga (to limber up those limbs), and spoiling their big red tomcat Tommy.

Sign up for the no-spam newsletter and be the first to know when a new book comes out: nicsaint.com/newsletter.

www.nicsaint.com

facebook.com/nicsaintauthor

twitter.com/nicsaintauthor

bookbub.com/authors/nic-saint

amazon.com/author/nicsaint

Printed in Great Britain
by Amazon

44915831R00139